"CAPTAIN," SCOTT SAID, "THEY'VE STRIPPED THE CONESTOGAS DOWN."

"How long to get one ready for inhabitants?"

"Three, maybe four days," Scotty said. "And that's without me doin' a full check of the environmental systems. How many ships are ya gonna be needin' again?"

"All the Conestogas," Kirk said. "And we have less than three days to get people to safety."

"Not possible, sir," Scott said. "Even if we found all the environmental equipment in one piece, it would take us weeks to get it all working again."

"It's going to have to be possible, Mr. Scott. Sixty thousand colonists may have no other choice. Kirk out."

Sulu frowned as Scott just shook his head.

Around Scott, the giant ship seemed even emptier than it had a moment before. This was one miracle he didn't think he could pull off for the captain.

STAR TREK®
NEW EARTH

BOOK FIVE OF SIX
THIN AIR

KRISTINE KATHRYN RUSCH
AND
DEAN WESLEY SMITH

NEW EARTH CONCEPT BY DIANE CAREY AND JOHN ORDOVER

POCKET BOOKS

New York   London   Toronto   Sydney   Singapore   Belle Terre

An *Original* Publication of POCKET BOOKS

POCKET BOOKS, a division of Simon & Schuster Inc.
1230 Avenue of the Americas, New York, NY 10020

STAR TREK is a Registered Trademark of Paramount Pictures.

A VIACOM COMPANY

This book is published by Pocket Books, a division of Simon & Schuster Inc., under exclusive license from Paramount Pictures.

ISBN: 0-671-78577-X

First Pocket Books printing August 2000

10 9 8 7 6 5 4 3 2 1

Printed in the U.S.A.

For Jim Kiser and Judy Joyce
Good Friends

Chapter One

THE CLEAR CANISTER sitting on the *Enterprise* science lab bench held no more than a few handfuls of brown soil, taken directly from a field just outside of Belle Terre's main colony on the island side of the planet. It was farm soil, nothing more. Recently tilled, the soil smelled of rich possibilities, seasons full of fresh, crisp vegetables, and the very future of Belle Terre.

Only there was something very wrong with this soil. And Spock was trying to figure out exactly what that was.

On the counter beside the canister were almost two dozen other canisters, all containing soil from different areas of Belle Terre. The soil from the explosion-blasted side of the planet seemed darker, almost black with the radiation damage from what the colonists were calling "the Burn." Two canisters seemed almost to be full of light sand.

But, from what Spock had been told, areas of soil around the planet were "going bad," as the colonists put it. Plants were dying, and in places the soil even smelled foul and rotten. Lilian Coates had asked Captain Kirk to look into it, and the captain had assigned Spock to help the colonist scientists discover what was wrong.

All the soil canisters in the lab were carefully labeled and sorted by region and continent. It had taken three *Enterprise* crew members most of a day to collect all of them for Spock. And he had spent the last two hours analyzing the data from scans of each sample. His findings had not been what he had expected. The soil contained polymers that just didn't belong logically on Belle Terre, let alone in every sample from every region of the planet.

Spock held his tricorder over the sample of rich soil from the largest island on the undamaged side of Belle Terre, then inserted a small silver probe into the soil. He again checked the readings of the soil, then stepped back and flipped a switch on a nearby panel, sending a slight jolt of electricity into the soil through the probe. What he had expected from his readings was a small puff of smoke as the electrical jolt broke down unknown gel molecules he had discovered in the soil.

That wasn't want he got.

The soil sample exploded with the force of a large bomb.

The impact smashed Spock back against the wall, knocking the wind from him. The room swirled with smoke and Spock's ears rang. He could feel a dozen cuts and gashes on his body from flying glass and debris.

He ignored the wounds, the shortness of breath, and his damaged ears and forced his attention completely on the explosion. He had not expected it, and did not know why it had happened. Simple farming soil did not normally explode when touched with electricity. Clearly the soil problem developing on Belle Terre was far worse than he had first thought.

Alarm bells were sounding throughout the ship as he slowly stood.

"Spock! Spock! Come in." Captain Kirk's voice carried over the alarms.

Spock stumbled a few steps through the glass and debris, and tapped the comm link on the wall. "Spock here, Captain." His own voice sounded hollow and distant in his ears, and he had to lean against the wall for support.

The captain's voice came back instantly. "Spock, what happened? Are you all right?"

Spock looked through the smoke at the completely destroyed science lab, then said, "I fared better than the science lab. And I made a discovery."

"What?" Kirk demanded as two emergency personnel shoved the jammed door aside and rushed into the lab. They stopped, clearly stunned at the destruction; then one moved toward him as the other moved to stop the small fire in a panel.

Spock understood the men's reaction. He was surprised as well by the force of the explosion. He had grossly miscalculated and it had cost them a lot of important scientific equipment. It was equipment that would not be easily replaced this far from Federation space. It was also lucky that he had been the only person in the lab at the time. A human would have had little chance of surviving such an explosion.

At that moment Dr. McCoy shoved in through the half-open door and glanced around. "For the love of—" He instantly moved toward Spock, his medical tricorder in his hand. "What in green-blooded blazes have you done?"

"Spock?" Kirk demanded over the comm as McCoy scanned him. "What discovery?"

"Belle Terre is in trouble, Captain," Spock said.

"Explain," Kirk said.

"Jim," McCoy said to the comm unit on the wall before Spock could say a word, "if you want to talk to your first officer, it's going to have to be in sickbay."

McCoy waved over the two emergency crewmen to help him with Spock.

"I can walk, Doctor," Spock said, pushing himself away from the wall.

"I doubt that," McCoy said, his voice not hiding his disgust. "But you are more than welcome to try."

Three stumbling, painful steps later Spock realized the logical choice was to have help getting to sickbay. In fact, it was the only choice.

Spock was thankful that McCoy had the good sense not to say "I told you so."

Lilian Coates awoke with a start, gasping for air, sweat dripping from her forehead, her hair stuck to her cheeks. What an awful nightmare.

She looked around her bedroom, trying to get something familiar back while forcing herself to take a few deep breaths. That was the worst dream she had had since right after the Burn. For the weeks after that she had dreamed she was back in the cave with the children, trying to save them, but always failing. Luckily, in real life, she had been successful. She, her son, Reynold, and five other children had ridden through the explosion of the planet's olivium-filled moon inside a cave. After a month or so the nightmares of Reynold dying, just as her husband had done, ended. But the memory of them always seemed just below the surface of every minute of every day.

She took another long, deep breath and blew outward, letting the fresh air clear her mind. Then she swung out of bed and in the faint light she padded to Reynold's room, glancing in at him. Their cat, Nova, a gift from Dr. McCoy, lay curled around Reynold's feet. Both seemed to be sleeping fine, so she moved on into the kitchen area, trying not to think about the nightmare until she calmed down some.

A large glass of cold water helped and she sat at the kitchen table still cluttered with a few dishes left from last night's dinner with Reynold and Captain Kirk. Jim had returned to his ship shortly after dinner and she just hadn't felt like cleaning up. Right now she wished he were here. Someone to talk to, someone to tell her that staying on Belle Terre, not going back to Earth, was the right thing to do for her and Reynold.

Slowly she let the nightmare back into her thoughts. *She is outside, standing in her garden, under clear,*

5

sunny skies. Around her all her plants are dead and wilted. Suddenly her feet become rooted to the soil, as if she is a plant as well.

She can't move.

Then she feels pressure around her face, as if someone is putting a hand over her nose and mouth, choking off her air. But there is no one there.

She can't run.

She can't breathe.

She is dying, just as her garden is dying.

Reynold is beside her, also planted, also unable to breathe.

She can't save him either.

She knew they were about to suffocate when she awoke.

Awful nightmare.

Another long drink of water pushed the images back again. It seemed she was more worried about her garden, and other plants around the area, than she had even told Jim. No doubt the plants dying had something to do with the Burn and the extreme changes in climate and weather. She knew there was a logical explanation for it.

But it seemed her subconscious didn't.

She glanced at the time. Two hours until she and Reynold had to be up. There wasn't going to be any getting back to sleep now. Not after that nightmare. She stood and picked up the last of the dishes from last night's dinner and moved to the sink, where she could wash them.

She was the school administrator for the colony and

librarian. She had more than enough work to keep her busy.

Two hours later, as she fixed her and Reynold's breakfast, the nightmare still haunted her, like a shadow she didn't want.

And looking at the slowly wilting plants in her garden as she and Reynold headed off to school, she knew that part of the nightmare was truth. The question that worried her was, *Which part?*

Governor Pardonnet smiled at Tegan Welch as if she were a child, giving her his best false smile. She desperately wanted to smash it into his face. It was that smile that had at first convinced her to trust the man, to follow him for light-years to this planet. And it was that smile that was condemning her son, Charles, to death.

She was a short woman, at best five feet one inch tall, but she knew how to fight and defend herself and her son. She stepped right up close to him, staring up into his face, forcing him to step backward in the tight space of the medical lab. "Take a look in that room again, Governor." She pointed to a closed door. "My son and four others are going to die unless you get us back to Federation space."

"I understand that, Ms. Welch," Pardonnet said, trying to ease sideways from where she had him pinned against a medical stand. The small medical supply room was no bigger than a closet. It was where she had asked for a word privately with him the minute they learned the cause of the illness her son and the others were suffering from.

"So what ship are you planning to send and when?"

"We're going to get them to the hospital ship first," Pardonnet said, "now that we know the cause of their illness."

She shook her head. "Not enough and you know it."

All the doctors, including Dr. McCoy from the *Enterprise,* had been clear that the only way to save these people was to get them a long distance away from olivium and the subspace radiation it was emitting. After the explosion of the Quake Moon, olivium had pelted the planet and spread like a wave through the system. Her son and the four others were allergic to the standard radiation treatments—and all the others McCoy had been able to whip up. Deathly allergic.

Her son would die unless he was away from the olivium and she was going to make sure he got away from it, one way or another.

"We don't know that getting them to the medical ship won't be enough," Pardonnet said, anger in his voice as he pushed passed her, trying to get to the door. She moved to block his way.

Pardonnet stopped and stared at her. "Ms. Welch, getting your son out of the atmosphere might stop the spread of the reaction. On the medical ship we can get him and the others into a sterile, protected ward."

"And what exactly did Dr. McCoy say about that idea?" she asked.

Pardonnet stared and said nothing.

"It seems I remember him saying along the lines of 'That would work when pigs fly.' Am I correct?"

"Dr. McCoy can be wrong," Pardonnet said. "We're going to try it first, then face the next step."

"My son and the others' lives are not worth a ship to you, are they?"

Pardonnet actually looked stunned at the accusation; then his eyes hardened and he said, "I have sixty thousand lives to worry about every minute of every day. Now excuse me." He shoved past her and out into the ward.

She had been right. Five lives were not worth a ship to the governor.

She stood staring at the medical supplies for a moment. Somehow there had to be a way to get her son out of the deadly poison from the olivium and, ideally, back to Federation space. But just away from the olivium first.

And if there was a way, she was going to find it. The first step was getting Charles off the planet and to the hospital ship. From there she'd figure out what to do. If it meant stealing a ship and flying it herself, she'd do it. She just hoped it wouldn't come to that.

But if it did, she wouldn't hesitate.

Chapter Two

KIRK STRODE INTO SICKBAY, glancing at a preliminary damage report an ensign had handed to him in the hall. The science lab had pretty much been destroyed, as well as minor structural damage to the deck both above and below it. Very little of the equipment in the lab would be salvageable. From the looks of this report, Spock was lucky to be alive.

Very lucky.

McCoy was standing over his patient, sealing cuts and healing scrapes. From the looks of what was left of Spock's bloodied uniform, the Vulcan had more places on him cut and scraped than not. A large gash cut from just above his left eye to the middle of his forehead. McCoy had closed it, but the wound would still look nasty for some time.

"How is he?" Kirk asked, ignoring his first officer's failed attempt to push himself up on his elbows.

"He's going to live," McCoy said. "But only because he's lucky to be half Vulcan."

"There is no luck involved, Doctor," Spock said, again trying to rise. McCoy easily pushed him back and kept working on the cuts and scrapes on Spock's left arm.

Kirk moved up closer to the bed and looked down at his first officer. "What happened, Mr. Spock?"

"Can't this wait, Jim?" McCoy asked. "Let me at least stop all the bleeding."

Kirk looked at the cuts and scrapes on his friend, then nodded. "I suppose another few minutes—"

"It cannot wait, Doctor," Spock said. He raised his head enough to look Kirk in the eye. "The sample of soil taken from the south side of the main colony island exploded."

Before Kirk or McCoy could react, Spock continued. "To be more precise, a group of polymers contained in the soil sample expanded in an explosive fashion when struck with a charge of electricity of the intensity of a normal lightning strike."

"How?" Kirk asked. The colony on Belle Terre had been through enough already. Spock had simply been trying to discover what was causing crop failures in different areas. What had led him to this?

Spock pushed McCoy away for the moment and sat up, clearly not back to his normal self, but regaining at least enough strength to sit up.

McCoy just shook his head and moved around to the

11

other side, where he could work on Spock's back while he talked.

"I discovered," Spock said, "that in all the soil samples taken from different areas of the planet a polymerized chain of silicon dioxide molecules is forming."

"Silicon dioxide? Isn't that sand?" Kirk asked. "That's a basic in most soil samples."

"In its normal state, yes," Spock said. "But for an unexplained reason this polymerized chain of molecules is forming what is commonly called a 'siliconic gel.' When completely expanded, a cubic foot of this 'siliconic gel' would be almost invisible, and very brittle."

"Lighter-than-air soil," McCoy said, laughing. "Now I've heard of everything." McCoy tossed an instrument on a tray with a loud bang and picked up another, which he used to start sealing one cut on Spock's arm.

"It's not a laughing matter, Doctor," Spock said. "Siliconic gel was first discovered on Earth in your twentieth century, but deemed to be a fairly harmless discovery, since in nature the material never existed in large amounts."

"So what caused the explosion?" Kirk asked. He stared at his first officer. So far none of this was making much sense at all.

"This type of molecular structure, by its very nature, expands," Spock said, using his hands to show a slowly expanding circle. McCoy pushed his arm back down in annoyance as Spock continued.

"It can enlarge quickly to thousands of times its size when introduced to a certain stimulus, in this case an electrical current. In essence, Captain, the soil expanded in an explosive fashion to form the 'siliconic gel' instantaneously."

Kirk just stared at his first officer, not really wanting to believe what he had just heard. But the ruined science lab and ripped uniform and cuts on Spock were a clear indication of the seriousness of what Spock was saying.

"How much did you test?" McCoy asked. "Had to be a lot to do this much damage."

"Approximately half a standard beaker full, Doctor," Spock said.

"A handful of soil caused this much damage?" Kirk asked. The idea of that kind of power being contained in simple garden soil stunned him.

And then he thought of the garden outside of Lilian's house, and the idea of it exploding with that same amount of force, and he shuddered.

"Yes, Captain," Spock said.

"You said you found this siliconic gel forming in all the soil samples?" Kirk asked, trying to get his mind to wrap around the problem facing them.

"Yes, Captain," Spock said again. "More in some samples than others, but this phenomenon is clearly contaminating the entire planet."

McCoy stopped and stared at the Vulcan, clearly shocked.

Kirk was feeling the same way. "Why didn't we see this before now?"

"Because it wasn't there," Spock said simply.

"Caused by the moon explosion?" McCoy asked. "Or some of that olivium that plowed into the surface?"

"Possibly," Spock said. "But I do not **think so**."

"Then what caused this?" Kirk asked. "And what's going to happen?"

"I don't have enough evidence to point conclusively to an exact cause," Spock said, "but the inevitable result is clear. The siliconic gel will continue to form in one fashion or another, either slowly or explosively, and the planet will become uninhabitable."

"What?" McCoy shouted, turning Spock so he could look into his eyes. "You can't be serious."

Spock only looked at the stunned face of Dr. McCoy without saying a word.

Kirk knew exactly how McCoy was feeling. After all they had gone through, they couldn't lose this planet now, so close to the *Enterprise* turning guardianship over to the *Starship Peleliu*, due to arrive within weeks. Not after what the colonists have gone through to get the planet settled. Not after what they had all gone through to save it.

"Why will it become uninhabitable?" McCoy demanded. "I'm not following you."

"As I said, Doctor, siliconic gel, when completely expanded, is a large, fragile construct. It will appear clear, much like regular air, but it is really highly expanded silicon molecules. In essence, a very thin type of glass."

"So what will happen then?" Kirk asked, afraid he knew the answer.

Spock looked first at McCoy, then at Kirk before he went on. "The siliconic gel, being, despite what the Doctor said, slightly heavier than air, but far more dense, will shove the breathable air out of the way. Eventually, the bottom five miles of atmosphere will contain nothing but this siliconic gel substance, destroying all life."

"Oh," McCoy said, stunned.

"How long?" Kirk asked.

"No way to say exactly, Captain," Spock said.

"Speculate," Kirk said. He needed a time frame on this.

"A number of days in some areas before the situation becomes critical," Spock said, "a few weeks in others, maybe even a month in the less-infected areas. There are too many factors involved to give an exact time. With the right stimulus, as I discovered in the lab, some areas of the planet are ready to explode now."

"Are you saying that one good lightning storm could wipe out an entire area of Belle Terre?" McCoy asked.

"That is exactly what I am saying, Doctor."

Kirk shook his head. His mind wasn't completely accepting what Spock was saying. Not after all they had done here, they couldn't lose Belle Terre this way.

"Can it be stopped?" Kirk asked.

"I do not even know how it started, Captain," Spock said. "Answering your question is impossible without further data and study."

Kirk looked at his cut and banged-up science officer, then at McCoy. "Bones, get Spock fixed up, then both of you meet me on the bridge."

He turned and headed for the door. Right now there were sixty thousand colonists on that planet and he had their safety to think about first and foremost. And that meant two things. Getting the Conestoga ships back up and running so the colonists would have somewhere to go. And the telling Governor Pardonnet exactly what they had found.

Telling him was one thing, getting him to believe him and act was another.

Chief Engineer Montgomery Scott stood in the middle of the engine room of the giant Conestoga and just shook his head. This was his last stop on a quick inspection tour of the ship, and it was as bad as the rest. Seemingly everything had been stripped and sent to the surface.

Captain Kirk had sent him and Sulu to do a quick check of this ship to learn what it would take to get the ships ready to house the population of Belle Terre. Sulu was to meet him here in the engine room, but it looked as if Scott was the first to arrive.

In his quick walk-through of the ship, Scott had discovered the bedrooms were bare, with even the closet bars removed. The kitchens that had fed thousands for months were nothing more than rooms full of holes where equipment had fit into walls. Hallways were stripped of wiring and panels. In many places even the flooring and wall coverings had been removed.

"Bridge stripped bare," Sulu said, as he came through the door. "Nothing left anywhere. Look at this," he said, stopping and pointing at the hole in the doorjamb where the door had been. "They even took the sliders. What would they use those for?"

"They took evrathin', laddie," Scott said.

"I suppose it makes sense," Sulu said, shaking his head, "assuming you never expected to use the ships again."

"Doin' this to a perfectly good ship is a crime," Scott said, and he believed it. Only now, it seemed, the colonists of Belle Terre were going to pay for this crime with their lives. And that just wasn't right.

"They left some things in here," Sulu said, looking around.

"Not much," Scotty said. "Equipment specific to the mule engines and smaller steerin' jets."

"Didn't have use for it on the surface, I bet," Sulu said.

"Kept the big ship in a steady orbit, laddie," Scott said, "and to cover up what they'd done."

Sulu nodded. "Makes sense. Hard to ignore big ships falling from orbit."

"That it would be," Scott said. He flipped open his communicator. "Scott to Captain Kirk."

"What'd you find, Scotty?" Kirk's voice came back instantly.

"Basically, sir," Scott said, staring around again, "nothin' but an empty hull. She'll stay in place, but that's about it."

"How about living quarters, kitchens, things like that?"

"Stripped barer than a polished dance floor," Scott said. "You gonna have people livin' here, they better bring their campin' gear and oxygen masks."

There was a long silence from the captain. Then he asked, "What exactly would it take for people to live on that ship in orbit? Give me some good news, Scotty."

"Food supplies, kitchens rebuilt, bathrooms rebuilt, and beds I suppose would get them by. The biggest problem would be to have all the environmental equipment put back and in working order as well."

"They took that, too?" Kirk asked, surprise sounding in his voice.

"As I said, Captain," Scott said, "they stripped her down like she was a goin' to the junk heap."

"How long to get one ready for inhabitants?"

"Three, maybe four days," Scotty said. "And that's per ship with a full crew workin' at her. And that's without me doin' a full check of the environmental systems. Might be worse. How many ships are ya gonna be needin' again?"

"All the Conestogas," Kirk said. "And Spock tells me we have less than three days in some areas to get people to safety."

"Not possible, sir," Scott said. "Even if we could find all the environmental equipment on the planet in one piece and just bring it back up to each ship, it would take us weeks to get it all working again."

"It's going to have to be possible, Mr. Scott. Sixty thousand colonists may have no other choice. Kirk out."

Sulu frowned as Scott just shook his head.

Around Scott, the giant ship seemed even emptier than it had a moment before. This was one miracle he didn't think he could pull off for the captain.

Chapter Three

GOVERNOR PARDONNET forced himself to slow down after he got outside the hospital and into the fresh, cool air of the morning. The sun was up, and even with a thin cloud cover, the coming day promised to be beautiful and warm. This area needed a few days like this to improve everyone's mood.

He strode down the gravel path in front of the hospital and turned toward the settlement center where he kept an office. Tegan Welch had gotten under his skin, of that there was no doubt. And he didn't blame her, with her son dying. But there were many factors she just didn't understand at the moment.

After the Burn, and the disasters that followed for the settlements along the Big Muddy, they were short of everything. They had cannibalized many of the ships for supplies and equipment. Not even Captain Kirk knew exactly how much they had taken out of those big ships still orbiting up there. Pardonnet wasn't even sure if he knew. On much of it he had simply looked the other way. His focus had been on getting the people settled safely on the surface and starting to mine the ore on land and from space. The explosion of the moon had seeded Belle Terre with olivium, but a large portion of the rare material had been blasted clear of the planet and into space.

Of course, some ships of the original wagon train had not been touched, which included the hospital ship, but any ship that could be used as an ore-chaser had been converted to one. Before they started taking parts and materials from the ships, he doubted there was a ship left under his control that could have safely handled the long trip back to Federation space. Now he was certain of it. And the five people who were allergic to the subspace properties of olivium would never survive a flight in an ore carrier, that close to that much of the stuff.

Tegan Welch also didn't know that in a month or so Kirk and the *Enterprise,* plus a few of the other Starfleet ships, were due to head back. If, on the hospital ship, the doctors could find a way to keep the Welch kid and the others alive that long, then Pardonnet was sure that Kirk would take them with him. There were a lot of things Pardonnet didn't like about Kirk, but he had to admit, the man cared a lot about people.

The clouds and sky were still faintly red from all the dust and remains from the Burn, but it seemed to be clearing a little every day. And slowly the weather patterns were starting to settle down some, especially on the main continent. Belle Terre, given enough time, was going to be a beautiful place to live again. And with all the olivium, a very rich place as well.

Ahead of him his assistant, Mary, wearing a blue dress and running shoes, rushed from the log building that was his office. She looked up the street at him and waved for him to hurry, moving at almost a run to meet him.

He didn't pick up his pace. After the conversation with Ms. Welch, he didn't feel like being rushed for anything.

Mary had a look of worry on her face, but she often did. She had become his assistant after the floods, when it became clear that he needed help to run a colony of sixty thousand people spread over an entire planet. Mary was efficient, fairly young at twenty-three, and didn't mind working long hours, but there was no doubt he was going to need more help very soon. The work was starting to overwhelm the both of them.

"Governor," Mary said when she was a dozen paces from him. "Captain Kirk is looking for you. He said it's urgent."

Pardonnet laughed and kept walking at the same pace toward the office, letting Mary fall into step beside him. "Kirk always says something is urgent. Haven't you learned that by now?"

"This time he seemed even more demanding than normal," Mary said.

Pardonnet laughed again as he turned in to the office, a medium-sized log building built first as a medical shelter, then turned over to him when the hospital was built up the road. In a small side room was a communications board. During emergency times, the room was staffed around the clock. But there hadn't been anyone besides him and Mary using this room for a long time now.

Pardonnet reached the panel and flicked a switch. "Governor Pardonnet to *Enterprise*. Come in."

"Governor," Kirk said, his voice coming back clear and very quickly, "are you in your communications room?"

"I am," Pardonnet said.

"Good," Kirk said.

Pardonnet glanced at Mary and shrugged. He started to ask Kirk what he wanted when suddenly a transporter beam took him, leaving Mary standing, her mouth open in surprise.

"Damn you, Kirk!" Pardonnet said aloud. Kirk wasn't going to get away with this. Not this time.

Two young *Enterprise* crew members in maroon uniforms greeted him in the *Enterprise* transporter room as the beam released him. Both looked very serious.

"This way, Governor," one said, turning toward the door.

"And if I don't want to go?" Pardonnet asked, stepping down off the transporter platform and looking at the man who stood in the door.

"With apologies, Governor, Captain's Kirk's orders are to take you in any fashion that is necessary. Sir."

Pardonnet nodded, containing his anger. In all the times they had worked together, Kirk had never pulled anything like this before. He'd better have one damned good reason, or he was going to have more problems than he could ever imagine.

Pardonnet followed the young crew member with the

rifle to a door labeled SCIENCE LAB, then stood aside and indicated Pardonnet should enter.

The door was broken and shoved back. Pardonnet stepped inside and looked around. He was alone and the place smelled of chemicals and smoke. A couple of portable lights had been set up, illuminating the space. Clearly the room had been destroyed by a fairly large explosion just recently. There didn't look to be anything larger than half a chair remaining intact. And glass and equipment were scattered everywhere.

Captain Kirk stepped into the room behind him, his boots making crunching noises in the broken glass. Kirk was followed quickly by Dr. McCoy and the Vulcan Spock. Spock clearly looked as if he'd been in the explosion, with cuts on his face and exposed hands.

"I'm waiting for an explanation of my kidnapping," Pardonnet said, stepping toward the captain. "I assume it has something to do with the explosion that happened here."

"It does," Kirk said. "An electrical charge sent into a small sample of soil from a garden outside of the main colony compound exploded, causing this damage."

Pardonnet's first reaction was to laugh, and he did. Captain Kirk, Dr. McCoy, and Spock did not return the laughter.

"Come on, Captain," Pardonnet said, "you can't be serious. Why would soil explode?"

"Oh, I'm very serious," Kirk said. "And the soil did explode. I wanted you to see this. Spock, explain to the governor what is happening as we head back to the bridge."

Kirk turned and strode for the broken door, followed by McCoy.

By the time they reached the bridge, Spock had explained the properties of siliconic gel, had explained how it was forming, had explained the explosive nature of the substance, and had even suggested that the planet needed to be evacuated.

"Evacuated?" Pardonnet asked as Spock moved to his science station and Kirk stood next to his own command chair. "Again? Your solution to all our problems is to run away."

"That's hardly fair, Governor," Kirk said. "I've worked hard to make certain you could stay. But it's my job to tell you when to prepare to run."

"My apologies," Pardonnet said. "You're right. What planetwide disaster, exactly, do we face this time?"

"Siliconic gel is going to expand to fill the lower few miles or so of atmosphere in a very short time. It will suffocate all life in and under it. Unless we can find a way to stop it."

Pardonnet started to open his mouth to say something, but for the life of him, he couldn't think of anything to say. His stomach was twisting so hard he felt he wanted to be sick. And all he could think about was the useless Conestogas floating in orbit, cannibalized for parts. There were sixty thousand people on the surface with no means of escape.

If they died, it was going be his fault.

"Governor," Kirk said, "we're going to have to approach this on a dual front. While we are trying to stop the siliconic gel from forming, we had hoped that you could get the Conestogas restaffed and start getting people off the surface in case we fail."

Pardonnet looked at the captain, not saying anything. His gaze locked with Kirk's and the two stood for a moment; then Kirk started to understand, slowly, without a word being said.

"But that's not possible, is it?" Kirk said softly.

"What? Why not?" McCoy asked, glancing between the two of them.

"You authorized it, didn't you, Governor?" Kirk said, his words low and cold.

Pardonnet turned to McCoy, who was standing near him at the rail. "We've been cannibalizing the Conestogas for supplies and equipment on the surface, as well as parts for the ore ships."

"Dammit," Kirk said, turning away.

"None of them are operational?" McCoy asked, his anger clearly right on the surface as he stepped closer. "Where do you intend to put all those people?"

Pardonnet could only stand there and say nothing. There was nothing to be said.

"It would seem," Spock said after a moment of silence, "that finding a way to stop this siliconic gel has become critical."

McCoy glared at the science officer. "Sometimes, Spock, your ability to state the obvious astounds me."

"Thank you, Doctor," Spock said.

Pardonnet simply stared at the image of Belle Terre filling the lower corner of the main screen, its white clouds and oceans looking serene and peaceful. But it didn't seem that anything about this planet was peaceful.

The Kauld observation station hung in the blackness of space, just inside the Belle Terre system's Oort cloud. It was a hollowed-out asteroid itself, with no distinguishing markings on the outside to give it away. All energy signatures inside were blocked by heavy screening. To any passing ship, it was simply another asteroid to be avoided.

The observation post had only three full-time inhabitants, and a ship hadn't stopped at the station in over a month. Yanorada, the mind behind the coming destruction of Belle Terre, sat in a large comfortable chair in front of three large screens, thinking. At the moment all three screens were blank.

The other two Kauld with him were his two assistants, Relaagith and Ayaricon. The three of them were the only ones living on the asteroid. They had had no contact with Kauld now for almost two months.

Relaagith had just finished some minor repairs on the data-recording system when Ayaricon brought the three of them lunch.

"Just over one hour until the Blind," Ayaricon said, placing the food on a small table in the center of the room. "Yanorada, sir, you need to eat for energy."

Yanorada nodded, staring at the blank screens. The Blind, or Gamma Night, as the humans called it, would soon be on them all. The Blind, caused by two nearby orbiting neutron stars, blocked all forms of sensor and communications for ten hours of every thirty. During those hours the information from Belle Terre would flow to them on tight-focused lasers, cutting through the Blind interference on a preprogrammed targeting system. It was only during the Blind that he could be sure no one would discover where they were, so that was the only time he could find out what was happening on Belle Terre.

The other twenty hours they spent waiting and studying the data sent them. So far, the attack was going as he had planned. Months earlier, he had sent a stripped-down Kauld warship on a suicide mission to Belle Terre loaded with the microscopic agents that would start the siliconic gel formation in the top inches of Belle Terre's soil. Captain Kirk and his ship had done as expected, destroying the warship in the upper atmosphere of Belle Terre, insuring the wide spread of the formation agents. Soon their precious colony would be a lifeless hunk of rock and the humans would be dead and gone. And then he would be the hero of his people.

He would have done what Vellyngaith and his warships and his stupid laser beam could not do. He would have destroyed the human colony.

He stood and moved to the food, making himself take a small portion, then returning to his chair. The last report had the siliconic gel forming nicely in most areas of the planet. He was so excited to see the new reports coming in shortly, he could barely force himself to eat. Two, maybe three more Blinds and his mission would be over and he could leave this hellish observation rock and return home as a hero.

Humans dead. Success. It was going to be wonderful

to return home and look into the eyes of Vellyngaith and just smile.

Kirk turned to stare at Governor Pardonnet.

"And you knew this was happening?" McCoy demanded, before Kirk could say anything. It seemed that McCoy was even angrier than he was.

"Some of it I ordered," Pardonnet said, not looking into Kirk's or McCoy's gaze. "And I knew more was being done than I had given permission for. It wasn't too hard to notice equipment appearing on the surface that wasn't in any of the original supply lists."

Kirk nodded. Now that he thought back about it, he'd been curious a few times as well about certain equipment. But he hadn't cared enough to stop and put the pieces together. And now that he was calming down, he wondered if he would have even halted the scavenging if he had known about it.

"What were you thinking?" McCoy asked, clearly angry.

"These people have no intention of returning to Federation space, Doctor," Pardonnet said, now facing McCoy. "This is their home. Why keep a fleet of ships sitting uselessly in orbit when the parts and equipment would be helpful in starting the new settlements?"

"Because the ships may be needed," Bones said, stepping closer to the governor.

"When you were growing up on Earth, Doctor," Pardonnet said, not backing down from McCoy, "were there enough ships in orbit to evacuate your entire planet?"

"Of course not," Bones said, disgusted. "But Earth wasn't a colony."

"And this siliconic gel would be doing the same thing there as well as here," Pardonnet said.

"Okay," Kirk said, motioning for Bones to back off, "we know the situation and it can't be changed. Yelling about it isn't going to help. We work with what we have. Now we need to find some answers. Understood?"

Both men nodded and said nothing, so Kirk turned to his science officer. "Spock? Anything new?"

Spock turned from his station, the cut on his forehead looking sore and angry. "Possibly, Captain. I've managed to download my findings from before the explosion in the science lab." He nodded at the main screen.

An image of a complex molecular structure appeared there, spinning slowly so that it could be studied from all sides. To Kirk's untrained eye, it looked like nothing he'd ever seen before. The molecules were organized in a thin, lattice-like structure.

"This is what we are up against, Captain," Spock said. "The basic structure of the siliconic gel being formed in the soil. If this was a naturally occurring gel, it would be possible to synthesize a catalyst that would release the bonds between the molecules, allowing them to return to a normal shape and configuration."

Kirk stared at the screen, studying what he saw like he would study an enemy ship. "But I assume this isn't natural occurrence?"

"No, it isn't," Spock said. "Something is artificially creating these polymers, Captain, and the links between the molecules are stronger than anything I've ever seen before. A catalyst, if wrongly applied, would release energy instead of breaking the polymer down."

Kirk studied the image on the screen. How could something so simple be so deadly?

"Is that what caused the explosion in the lab?" Pardonnet asked.

Spock shook his head. "No, Governor. That explosion was caused by the almost instantaneous formation of billions of what you see on the screen. Such a reaction is typical for siliconic gel construction."

"Typical?" Pardonnet asked, puzzled. "Natural siliconic gel can explode as it did in your lab?"

Spock nodded. "Yes, it can, but it never exists in quantity. But I am more concerned about the solution after it is formed. Tearing apart of this siliconic gel, if done incorrectly, would release energy on a nuclear level. The result would be an explosion far more powerful than what happened in the lab."

There was a stunned silence on the bridge as they tried to soak in that information. Kirk started to pace near his command chair, two steps over, two back. Sometimes that helped him think.

"Back up for a second, Spock," McCoy said. "Are you saying that something is building these polymers?"

"Creating the base polymers in the soils that then leads to the formation of the siliconic gel, Doctor," Spock said. "It would be the only logical explanation. But I'm going to have to wait for more soil samples to find out exactly what is causing this unusual activity."

"Speculate, Spock," Kirk said, stopping his pacing at

the rail and staring intently at his first officer. "What is the most logical possibility?"

"Nanoassemblers, sir," Spock said. "Self-replicating. In essence, a mechanical virus spreading planetwide in the soil. A secondary option might be an artificial chemical reaction of some type. It would also spread in the same fashion."

"You mean this is an attack?" McCoy asked, clearly stunned.

Kirk had already come to the same conclusion, and he was betting on the Kauld being the ones doing the attacking. As Spock would say, it was the only logical conclusion.

"Basically, yes," Spock said.

"How long has this been going on?" Pardonnet asked.

"Speculation, again?" Spock asked.

Kirk nodded for his science officer to go ahead. Spock's speculations usually were better than many people's facts.

"From the rate of spread around the planet," Spock said, "from the extent of the siliconic gel creation in certain soils, using a standard rate of this kind of construction, and studying a few external factors, I would say it has been going on for three months, six days, twelve hours, and eighteen minutes."

Kirk looked at his science officer, completely stunned. Spock just stood there, his normal calm expression on his face, as if it was completely normal to speculate so precisely. But not even Spock's normal speculations were that accurate. There had to be something more Spock wasn't yet revealing that he knew.

"Now, that's some guess," McCoy said. "Remind me to take you to the Kentucky Derby some time. Bet you could guess the winner."

"Explain how you came to such an exact conclusion, Mr. Spock," Kirk ordered, ignoring McCoy.

"Yeah, tell us, Spock," Bones said, still laughing to himself.

"Using the basics I mentioned as to the spread of the siliconic gel, and the standard rate of construction of such a substance, I concluded the time that such a process started would be in the area of three to four months ago."

Kirk nodded. That sounded right to him as well.

Spock went on. "Using the theory of this event being artificially created, I studied the time period indicated for events that could possibly be related."

"The laser attack?" Kirk asked. "Nothing hit the surface of the planet during that."

"No," Spock said, then he faced McCoy. "Doctor, do you remember when Lilian Coates's child, Reynold, became sick after diving for what he thought was a meteorite?"

"Of course I do," Bones said. "What would that have to do with this?

Kirk also remembered the event clearly. McCoy had found nothing wrong with Reynold, and they had found nothing dangerous in the lake. But since he'd been spending time with both Lilian and Reynold lately, he'd often worried that whatever had caused Reynold to become sick might return again.

"That event could possibly tie it all together, Doctor," Spock said, pointing at the main screen. The image of the molecule disappeared to be replaced by a Kauld battle cruiser coming in at full speed toward Belle Terre.

"The suicide attack," McCoy said. "The day Reynold got sick near the lake."

"What suicide attack?" Pardonnet demanded.

"Just before we discovered the Kauld plan to destroy Belle Terre with a giant laser beam, a Kauld warship ran a suicide mission at Belle Terre. Nothing seemed to be related to it."

Pardonnet nodded. "Oh, right, I remember that. From the planet's point of view, Captain, it's hard to tell a suicide attack from any other."

The screen showed the *Enterprise* blowing the Kauld battleship out of space, just in the upper regions of the atmosphere. At the time the entire event had seemed very strange to Kirk, but then, with the discovery of the Kauld laser attack, the suicide attack had become forgotten before it could be investigated further.

Maybe, if the Kauld hadn't attacked with the laser, they would have discovered this attack in time to stop it.

Spock froze the image of the exploding Kauld battleship. "Captain, assuming that either of my assumptions, of nanoassemblers or a chemical agent, is correct, they did fire a weapon. The ship itself was the weapon and we were the planned detonating agent."

"We just didn't know it," McCoy said softly.

Kirk nodded. Now the suicide run of that Kauld warship was making sense.

"Spock," McCoy asked, "wouldn't the explosion of

the ship have destroyed the nanomachines, or the chemical?"

"I am only speculating at the moment, Doctor," Spock said. "But I do not think so."

"Continue speculating, Spock," Kirk said, staring at the frozen image of the exploding battleship.

"From the location of the Kauld ship's destruction," Spock said, "and considering prevailing conditions at the time in the upper atmosphere, the agents released by the Kauld would have spread over the entire globe. Where this ship exploded was in a perfect location for such spread."

"Planned very well, it would seem," Pardonnet said, the tone of disgust in his voice clear.

"More than likely," Spock said. "However, the atmospheric conditions, added with any remains of the ship that reached the surface, would create areas of higher concentrations of the chemical or nanoassemblers. The soil sample that exploded in the lab was taken near where Reynold Coates became sick."

"The meteorite that hit that lake was part of the Kauld ship?" Kirk asked.

Suddenly that event made sense as well. No wonder Reynold hadn't gotten sick again.

"Possibly," Spock said. "Again, I am only speculating at the moment. And the reason Reynold got sick could possibly have been simply lack of oxygen from being covered in the assemblers as they formed siliconic gel polymers around him."

"That would be consistent with his symptoms at the time," McCoy said. "No wonder he recovered so quickly."

"Keep working at it, Mr. Spock. I want to know the instant your speculations become fact."

"Understood," Spock said.

Kirk dropped down into his chair and stared at the frozen image of the Kauld battleship. The Kauld had not only had the plan of firing the laser, but just in case that didn't work, which luckily it hadn't, they had this backup plan. When were the Kauld ever going to leave Belle Terre alone?

"Captain," Pardonnet said, stepping down beside Kirk's chair. "What do we do next? Gamma Night is coming on quickly."

With one last look at the image of the exploding Kauld battleship, Kirk turned around. "Uhura, clear the screen. Standard image."

"Yes, sir," Uhura said.

Kirk looked up into Pardonnet's worried face. "Governor, what we're going to do is pull you and your people out of the fire one more time. I want all your scientists working to find out what is causing this, and sharing their information with Spock on a continuous basis."

"Understood," Pardonnet said.

"I want you and your people to find and take back to the Conestogas all the environmental equipment and kitchen equipment, then start stocking the ships in preparation for an evacuation. Work with Chief Engineer Scott on the rebuilding."

Pardonnet nodded, not happy with the idea of evacuating all the people again.

Kirk turned away from the governor. "Spock, can you supply the governor with maps of areas of least concentration of siliconic gel formation? We can buy some time by evacuating the most dangerous areas."

"Governor, you will have it as soon as the soil samples are gathered and studied," Spock said. "The process is already under way."

"You all right with that?" Kirk asked Pardonnet.

Pardonnet nodded. "Better to move to other areas of the planet than evacuate, Captain."

"I couldn't agree more," Kirk said. "Get everyone working and keep me informed. I'll do the same for you."

Pardonnet took a deep breath and smiled. "Thank you, Captain."

"Don't thank me just yet," Kirk said.

The governor nodded and headed for the door as Kirk stared at the beautiful image of Belle Terre below him. They'd almost lost this planet twice before. Why was he afraid that the third time was going to be the one they couldn't stop?

Tegan Welch stood beside her son's bed on the main medical ward of the *Brother's Keeper*. The room smelled musty and very unused. There were over a hundred beds, divided by small walls that could be pulled out or retracted for privacy needs. At the moment all were retracted, all the beds made neatly, and only the five beds near the main door were now occupied. Clearly there hadn't been any patients here for months.

Captain Skaerbaek, a tall, thin man with a full mustache and thinning hair, stood beside her. He wore his white Starfleet medical uniform with ease, as if it belonged on him. He had alive, green eyes and a smile that came easily.

At the moment Dr. Akins had Charles and the other four patients sleeping soundly. And an orderly was stationed nearby in case any of them needed anything. The doctor had told her and the rest of the families that the medical ward was shielded as well as anything could be. But he was certain it would take some time before they might see any change in the patients. Being in a deep allergic shock to olivium ore was not going to pass quickly, even when the olivium was removed from the equation.

Tegan wasn't sure the olivium was removed, from what she knew about the properties of the ore. She doubted very much if the ward's shielding could protect her son and the other four from the subspace problems of the olivium. But she was willing to be wrong, as long as her son didn't get any worse in the test.

"Let me show you to your quarters," Captain Skaerbaek said, easing her by the elbow away from Charles's bed. The other family members had all beamed down to the surface a short time before. She was the only one who had asked to stay aboard.

Tegan let the tall captain pull her away. As Dr. Akins had said, there was nothing she could do at the moment. But she could get ready for the next possible step. If this shielding didn't help Charles and the others, then she was determined to get them out of the system and away from any possible subspace emissions from the olivium ore.

And to do that, she needed to start understanding what was possibly available in the way of ships. Even if the governor wouldn't assign a ship to take them to safety, she was sure she could find one. And the best place to look was in orbit.

"Thank you, Captain," Tegan said as she walked beside him out of the ward and down a long, wide hallway. Everything was hospital white, and felt as if it should be bustling with activity. At the moment ghosts would be more at home walking this hospital hallway.

"You're more than welcome," the captain said. "And please, call me Bill. It's wonderful to have some people back on board again. I just wish it could be for different reasons."

"Healing my son is a very good reason," Tegan said, smiling up at the captain.

He laughed with her. "Putting it that way, you are very right. I hope this works."

"So do we all," Tegan said.

"Trust Dr. Akins," the captain said. "He's one of best there is."

"Where is everyone?" she asked. "Don't you have a full crew of Starfleet personnel?"

"Twenty-six of us full-time Starfleet doctors, engineers, and orderlies came along. The rest of the crew on the way here were colonists. Until we get ready to leave, most of my Starfleet crew rotates to the surface. At any one point there are usually only six of us on board."

"Wow," Tegan said, "this monster ship must really feel empty with only six crew."

"Very empty," the captain said, nodding. "I've heard echoes that should never be heard on a spaceship."

She laughed. She liked this man. Anyone who could make her laugh when Charles was sick was someone special. Maybe with a little luck, and some time, he might help her find a solution. "You live on the surface as well?"

"Nope," he said. "My first officer and I are always on board."

"Starfleet regulations?"

He laughed. "No, just good common sense." He stopped and pointed into an open door. "Here you are. Just a quick walk from your son."

She glanced inside the spacious quarters. Her luggage had been placed just inside the door. Compared with her and Charles's room on the way here from the Federation, this was massive. It looked even bigger than their house on the planet's surface. "Wow, who lived here?"

"Actually," the captain said, "Dr. Ellay, chief surgeon for the colony, stayed here with his wife and three children. Biggest suite on the ship."

"And your quarters?" she asked.

"Up two decks," he said, pointing toward a nearby lift. "And nowhere near as big. Would you like to join me and my first officer for dinner?"

Tegan glanced up at the warm smile of the captain. "I'd love to. Do I have time to change and check on Charles first?"

"More than enough time," he said. "I'll stop by here in one hour. How does that sound?"

"Perfect," she said. "Thank you, Captain."

"Bill," he said, smiling. "And the pleasure is all mine."

"Bill," she said, smiling back at him. "One hour."

She stepped inside as the captain turned away.

The door slid closed behind her and she was alone in the biggest stateroom she'd ever seen. She walked over and looked into the main bedroom, marveling at the size. She could imagine rooms like this on yachts, but not on Starfleet ships.

After a quick walk-through of the suite, she started to unpack. So far everything was perfect. Charles was getting the best medical help available, and the captain was a pleasant man who she had a feeling she was going to enjoy spending time with.

With luck, Dr. Akins would be right and the shielding would be enough for Charles to get better. And if that was the case, they could live right here until this ship, along with the other ships, headed back to the Federation. She was sure they would take her and Charles along.

But just in case the shielding didn't work for Charles, she was going to make sure Captain Bill Skaerbaek was completely and totally on her side.

Chapter Four

YANORADA WATCHED the information pouring across the three screens in front of him. The Blind had started and, just as it had done for months now, the information poured in over the tight-beam lasers to his computers, where it was unscrambled and fed across the screens in front of him.

At the moment he just wanted to clap his hands like a happy child. He had over a hundred sensors planted in different locations and soils of Belle Terre, all collecting data during the time between Blinds. Then, with the laser system focused directly at his asteroid a few moments before the interference of the Blind started, he was able to get all the gathered information when there was no chance of detection.

This time every sensor on Belle Terre showed evidence of the siliconic gel formation. Two areas, both near where parts of the warship had survived all the way to the surface, were about ready to explode. And when that happened, it would be enjoyable watching the humans scramble for safety like ants from a disturbed anthill. He wished that for that event he could be in low orbit. It wasn't possible, but he could dream.

Once an area of siliconic gel started, it would be like a hole in a dam sprewing water at an extreme pressure. Only it wouldn't be water spewing from the hole, but siliconic gel, an invisible, suffocating layer covering everything. Nothing would be able to block it, and the very existence of the siliconic gel flowing from the area would trigger other areas into increased siliconic gel production. Once a single location broke lose, it would be less than three days before the entire planet was covered in the siliconic gel.

And Vellyngaith and the others had laughed at his plan. They had thought the humans would be easy to kill, but he knew better. And he had been proven right so far. The others were no longer laughing, from his reports from home. Now they were simply waiting. And from the looks of the data flowing across the screens in front of him, they were only waiting to welcome him home as a hero.

He would be known as the Kauld who had defeated the humans without firing a single shot.

He turned to Relaagith, his number one assistant, who was monitoring data collected from the humans over the last "day" period. "Any sign the humans are aware of what is happening?"

Relaagith turned and shook his head, smiling. "Nothing at all. They only worry about their crops, without discovering why the plants are dying. Humans truly are stupid."

"And from my calculations," Ayaricon, his second assistant, said, "the first major siliconic gel eruption will occur near one of their main colonies in less than thirty of their hours. It will overwhelm the entire colony to a height taller than the largest trees within one hour of starting."

"So by the next Blind, it will have finally started," Relaagith said. "Is it possible to have a ship within range to record the event?"

"Patience," Yanorada said, going back to studying the data as they flowed past his eyes. "We have waited this long. There is no point in taking any chances now. Besides, we are the only ones who know how to stop the siliconic gel. We will stay safely hidden here until it is finished and every human is either dead, or leaving the system."

"Of course," Relaagith said. "But it is only natural to want to watch the results of our hard work."

"Oh, we'll watch the results," Yanorada said, smiling, "from the central position of the parade they will give in our honor for killing all the humans."

Both Relaagith and Ayaricon laughed at that wonderful thought.

Kirk stood in the lift, not-so-patiently waiting for it to deliver him to the right deck. He had hated Gamma Night from the first moment they had entered this area of space, and he hated it even more now, after all this time. For ten hours out of every thirty, the *Enterprise* and all the other ships in the area were frozen in space, not daring to move. Ten long hours of being basically blind and deaf to anything happening around his ship. Not even Spock, after months of trying, had been able to figure out anything that would really help the situation much at all. Sensors just didn't work very well.

So every twenty hours communications and movement in this area of space came to a halt, and they just sat and waited, as they were doing now. Kirk hated that more than anything. Most of the Gamma Nights over the last month he had tried to be on the surface, with Lilian Coates, or doing something to keep his mind off the helplessness of it all. But this time he didn't dare leave the ship or get sleep. And he couldn't even check to see if Lilian was all right. He just hoped her entire town was preparing to evacuate. From what Spock had said, right near her was the highest concentration of the siliconic gel polymers in the soil.

The lift came to a smooth halt and he strode off down the hallway, ignoring everyone he passed. At the moment he was just too angry to even try to be friendly. Spock had done a complete analysis of the Kauld battleship that had exploded months before in the upper atmosphere. The ship had been full of hundreds of billions of self-replicating nanoassemblers. By the *Enterprise* doing what seemed to be the right thing and blowing the Kauld warship apart, they had simply released the nanoassemblers to float on the upper atmosphere, setting to work forming siliconic gel when they came into contact with the right substances.

He had been a Kauld pawn and they had played him perfectly. Kirk hated to be played with. It made him angry.

Gamma Night made him angry.

Being faced with a situation that was going to destroy something he had worked hard to build was making him even angrier. He and Spock and the scientists on the surface had the ten hours of Gamma Night to figure out a way to save the colony, save Belle Terre, and pay the Kauld back. And pay them back he would do.

During the time right before Gamma Night had set in, thirty soil samples from different areas of Belle Terre had been delivered to the *Enterprise*. Spock had set up a temporary lab in a mess area and filled it with what equipment he could find.

As Kirk entered the makeshift lab, he could smell sulfur and the faint odor of oranges. The soil samples were in open containers on a counter, looking more like bombs to Kirk than anything else. Spock was bent over a counter, looking into a scientific scope of some sort while at the same time typing in numbers on a keypad.

"Any luck, Mr. Spock?"

Spock glanced up. "I am endeavoring to keep luck out of this process, Captain."

"Results, Spock?" Kirk asked, forcing himself to take a deep breath. "What results have you gotten?"

"A number of smaller findings," Spock said, turning away from the scope and clicking on a monitor. He motioned for Kirk to look.

An image of the land surface of Belle Terre appeared. Kirk was more than familiar with it after all this time. The larger continent had been hit extremely hard during the explosion of the moon. Some of the colonists had decided to move back to that area anyway, while others picked the less damaged, but smaller, island chain on the other side of the planet.

The largest of those islands was where the main colony headquarters had relocated, and where Lilian and Reynold lived.

Spock indicated the screen. "The red shows the highest, and most dangerous, areas of siliconic gel polymer concentrations in the surface soil. Using the samples, I've extrapolated this map from wind and soil conditions."

The main colony island was a bright red. Kirk couldn't take his eyes away from it. It was as if the entire island were painted with blood.

"The blue indicates the safest areas," Spock said. "I was able to get this information to Governor Pardonnet before the onset of Gamma Night."

Kirk nodded. "How much time do the red areas have? The main colony area?"

"Less than twenty-four hours," Spock said.

"And then what will happen exactly?" Kirk asked. "If we can't stop it."

"Captain, it is already happening," Spock said. "The siliconic gel is forming in all of these soil samples."

Kirk glanced at the beakers sitting on the tables. "I don't follow you."

Spock moved over to one of the beakers. "Put your hand in the soil."

Kirk hesitated. He'd seen what a soil sample explosion had done to the science lab. He wasn't really that thrilled to have his hand at the explosion point.

Then with a look at his science officer's calm, passionless face, he put his hand down into the soft, cold soil.

"Feel the soil give and seem to shrink under your touch?" Spock asked.

Kirk nodded. It was a very weird sensation. It was as if he could take a handful of soil, move it around, and it would become less than a handful. "That's very strange, Spock. What's happening?"

"You are breaking down the siliconic gel molecules by simply moving the soil," Spock said.

Kirk pulled his hand out of the soil and grabbed a towel off the counter to wipe his hand off. "So you are saying that the volume in each of these beakers is increasing as we speak?"

"In essence, yes," Spock said. "Simply put, smaller, more compact molecules are being replaced by air-gel molecules, which are very expansive in nature. The mass isn't expanding, but the volume needed to contain the same amount of mass is."

"I'm still not completely following you," Kirk said. "What's going to happen within twenty-four hours on the main colony island?"

"The top six inches in soil over the entire area will have expanded to a height of twenty feet, Captain. It will be a clear, brittle layer that will push the breathable air above it, but no one will be able to walk on the new substance; thus any creature left on the surface and not protected will suffocate."

The thought of Lilian and Reynold, surrounded by a

clear, brittle substance, choking for air, made Kirk shiver.

"No explosion, then?" Kirk asked, trying to clear the images out of his mind.

"There will be many explosions," Spock said, "as some stimulus triggers a sudden expansion of the siliconic gel, as happened in the lab. However, without such stimulus, the siliconic gel polymers are expanding geometrically."

Spock pointed at the soil sample Kirk had put his hand into. "If left alone, that single sample would expand to fill this room. It will take forty-six hours to fill the beaker it is in. Only twenty more minutes after that to fill the entire room."

"What can we do to stop this?" Kirk asked, now finally understanding exactly what was going to happen.

"There are two logical ways of approaching this problem," Spock said. "We either stop the nanoassemblers from multiplying and creating new siliconic gel polymers, or we find a way to break down the siliconic gel as it is created."

Kirk looked at his first officer. If he was understanding what Spock was saying, even if they could find a way to stop the nanoassemblers, there was another problem. "We have to do either solution on a planetwide scale, don't we?"

"Exactly," Spock said. "The Kauld had the time and natural winds of the planet to spread the assemblers. We do not have such a luxury."

Kirk glanced back at the screen showing the red-covered island where the largest colony settlement was.

"So what do we do to stop it, Spock?"

"I do not know, Captain."

That just wasn't the answer he wanted to improve his mood.

Lilian Coates stood with her back against the wall in the large assembly hall and listened to Governor Pardonnet say the words she never thought she would have to listen to again.

"Prepare to evacuate."

The idea just made her head swim. This was her home, her planet. How could she and everyone else just be told they had to leave? She wished it weren't Gamma Night, so Jim could explain what was happening. Governor Pardonnet sure wasn't having much luck at it.

She fanned herself, trying to stay cool. The room's environmental controls couldn't handle this many people being crammed into the one space. Just weren't designed for it.

She could tell from the reactions of others in the main room that she wasn't the only one who didn't understand what Pardonnet was trying to say. She wasn't even sure if Pardonnet himself did. Their young, energetic governor was looking older and very tired.

"Look," Pardonnet shouted as fifty people tried to ask him questions at once, "I don't know most of the answers. All I know is that everyone on this island needs to be ready to evacuate the moment Gamma Night lifts. We'll move to the south to start with. If no solution has been discovered in a few days, we'll have to go back to the Conestogas."

"Governor," one man down front shouted, "you know those ships have been cannibalized for supplies."

Lilian shoved herself away from the wall. "What?"

She wasn't the only one around the room that didn't know that piece of information. A lot of people started shouting at once.

"We're dealing with that at the moment," Pardonnet said, holding his hands up to get people to calm down. "Just get ready. Meeting adjourned."

Instantly the room's noise level increased by a hundredfold as everyone turned to talk to the person beside them. Lilian didn't feel much like talking, so she just ducked out the door and headed into the warm sun toward her home. Even in the sunlight, it was cooler than inside. And the air was much fresher.

What did the man mean the Conestogas had all been cannibalized? Did that mean there was no escaping if they needed to? If so, why was the governor even talking about using the ships again?

She let the fresh air clear her mind.

The last time Pardonnet had given the order to evacuate, her son Reynold had been missing. She was going to make sure that didn't happen again this time. She and Reynold were going to stick together, no matter what happened.

She reached the sidewalk up to her front door. Her garden seemed even more wilted than it had been before she left, even though she knew that wasn't possible. But knowing there was possibly something in the soil that was killing her plants made it seem that way.

She went inside and looked around. A quick check

confirmed that Reynold was working on homework in his room. Everything was just so normal, so familiar.

She went back into the living room and dropped onto her couch. How was she going to be able to give up the cozy room where she and Jim had spent many an evening during Gamma Nights sitting and just reading?

She let herself think back over those evenings. He was comfortable to be with, and he had said the same about her. That fact seemed to have surprised them both. She still wasn't ready to get into another relationship, especially with a famous starship captain, but they enjoyed each other's company so much, it seemed as if they had just fallen into it.

Now, if they had to leave, those evenings in this room would end. She didn't like that thought at all.

She stood, moved to the kitchen, and got herself a glass of water. This was her second home since reaching Belle Terre. The first had been on the main continent, and had been completely destroyed in the moon explosion. She was proud of this one, much more than the first prefab dome that had been her and Reynold's first home. This one she had helped build with her own hands, out of wood from nearby forests. For some reason, that made it more hers.

Giving it all up wasn't going to be easy. In a whole lot of ways.

And the school. She'd helped build that, too. What would happen to the equipment and supplies at the school? If the evacuation was rushed, they were going to have to leave a lot of supplies behind.

But the machines, all the disks of knowledge,

shouldn't be left. She could get her and Reynold's bags packed quickly; then the two of them, maybe with help from other kids and a few adults, might be able to get much of the equipment and supplies ready to move as well.

She glanced at the time. Eight and a half hours until the end of Gamma Night. Not much time, but maybe enough to save what she considered the most important aspect of the colony. Knowledge.

She finished off her glass of water and then headed for Reynold's room. It was going to be a challenge to get ready in time, but maybe, if she could make it interesting enough for Reynold and the other children, she might get it done.

At least worrying about getting the school materials ready to move would keep her from thinking too much about losing her home.

And losing Belle Terre.

Chapter Five

TEGAN'S DINNER with Captain Skaerbaek just hadn't happened. Thirty minutes after he had left her in the large suite, the captain had called her over the communication link in her room. It seemed a situation had come up and he would have to take a rain check on dinner. He hadn't said anything more and she hadn't pressed him.

Her suite had its own small kitchen and at a quick glance she knew someone had stocked it with enough food to last for a week. She had then changed into comfortable clothes and gone back to the medical ward to sit by Charles.

At seven, before he got sick, Charles had been a spirited boy, with a smile that could light up a room and enough energy to power a ship. Now all she wanted was to have that boy back, not the sickly one sleeping here now.

Twenty minutes later, while sitting with her son, she learned from Dr. Akins what the captain's situation was. It seemed that for some strange reason caused by the Kauld, it might be necessary, after the Gamma Night was over, to evacuate the entire planet. There was a chance that all of Belle Terre might become uninhabitable.

Tegan pretended to be shocked, but all she really wanted to do was clap her hands and shout for joy. Belle Terre to her and Charles had become a prison. And a deadly poisonous place for Charles, with his allergy to olivium ore. If the entire colony was forced to leave, then Charles would get better.

But one hour later, still sitting beside Charles's bed, watching him breathe raggedly, she had decided she needed to continue with her plan to find her own way away from this system for her and Charles. Just in case Governor Pardonnet and his people were successful in finding a way to stay in this system. Charles didn't have the time. A few days, if the shielding in this hospital ship didn't work, might be too long for her son. And she wasn't going to just sit there and watch her son die.

She tucked the blanket around Charles and headed out of the main ward and down the hall toward her suite. But instead of going in, she just kept going. She knew her way around starships enough to know how they were laid out. And before coming to the *Brother's Keeper,* she had looked up a floor plan of the large hospital ship and studied it.

She had to admit, it was an impressive ship. If needed, the *Brother's Keeper* could care for over one hundred critically sick or wounded and another five hundred in the wards. It carried a crew and medical staff of another hundred when fully staffed. There were six stations on the bridge and five in engineering, plus massive storage and cargo holds.

But what interested her the most were the medical ship's shuttles. There were two of them, both parked in a large shuttlebay. Both shuttles had been used to help save Belle Terre in the moon explosion, but she doubted they had been used much since.

Both shuttles had enough power to get her and Charles away from the system if needed. And she thought she knew how to fly them, after being trained on small shuttlecraft back on Earth before joining this colony. Since her training she hadn't had the need or opportunity to fly a shuttle, but she doubted she had forgotten the skill.

Where she would take Charles she didn't know. There was no way a small shuttle could even begin to make the long trip back to Federation space. But just anywhere outside the influence of the olivium was all Charles needed. How she would get a shuttle out of the medical ship and away without detection, she also didn't yet know. At the moment she was just looking at options.

And taking one of those shuttles was an option.

With luck, Belle Terre would have to be abandoned and all the colonists would have to leave, taking her and Charles with them. That would serve the cold-hearted Governor Pardonnet just fine, as far as she was concerned.

She didn't meet anyone in the hallway to the shuttlebay, and the door to the bay slid open as she approached it, bringing the lights up inside automatically.

Her heart leaped at the sight of the two shuttles, both turned and waiting to be taken out of the wide shuttle-bay doors to space. The closest ship was called *Little Brother* and the other *Little Sister*.

"Cute names," she said out loud, her voice echoing in the large bay. She stepped forward toward *Little Sister* and the door closed behind her. She had always hoped to give Charles a little sister some day, when she found a new partner. Maybe this was a good sign.

She walked around the shuttle, making sure not to touch anything, pretending to be just a visitor gawking at a small ship, in case anyone was watching on a security camera. But her walk-around was enough to let her know the shuttle was in good working order, cleaned and more than likely ready to fly. Typical Starfleet preparedness.

"Beautiful," she said out loud, again her voice echoing.

With a smile at *Little Sister*, she headed out of the shuttlebay. Option one found. Now to see if she could prepare an option two. And that option concerned the captain.

"Impossible, sir," Scott said to Captain Kirk. "There is just no way those big ships will be ready, Capt'n. Not in ten days, let alone ten hours."

Kirk stared at his chief engineer. Scotty had spent the entire Gamma Night stuck on one of the Conestogas, climbing through everything, trying to fix what he and his crew could fix with limited parts. After a few hours inside the environmental controls, Scotty had said he knew it wasn't going to be possible. So the moment the Gamma Night had ended, he had beamed back to the *Enterprise* to tell the captain in person. Now, as Captain Kirk and Spock faced him in the science lab, the cannisters of soil seemed to dominate the room behind them.

Kirk was surprised, actually, at what Scotty was saying. It wasn't often his chief engineer said something couldn't be done. Period.

"Why?" Kirk asked. "What changed?"

"Them environmental systems, Capt'n," Scotty said. "Everythin's been completely torn out. It would take a complete rebuild and ya know that would take some time. I have my men checkin' to see if all the big ships are the same, but I have a sneakin' hunch they are."

"Sixty thousand colonists trapped on the surface," Kirk said, shaking his head. "Scotty, we have no choice."

"I'm sorry, Capt'n," Scotty said. "With a full crew, an' three full days, we might be able ta rebuild one or two of the ships, but that would be the best we could do."

"That wouldn't be enough," Kirk said. Even with cramming people on two ships, the other Starfleet ships, and the *Enterprise,* there was no way sixty thousand people could be taken care of. It was an impossible situation.

"There may be another option, Captain," Spock said.

"I'm listening," Kirk said. At this point, he was willing to listen to any ideas at all. They had to find a way to save the colonists and buy some time to stop this siliconic gel.

"Mr. Scott," Spock said, "the main components of the environment systems from each of the big ships were removed and taken to the surface of the planet, correct?"

"I dona know where else they'd have gone," Scott said.

"So, Captain," Spock said, "we could use those same

systems on the surface to protect the people there, instead of in the ships."

Kirk stared at his science officer, trying to understand what exactly Spock was saying. "How could that be done, Spock?"

"Build protective coverings," Spock said, "over the inhabited areas. They would only have to serve to hold the siliconic gel outside. And the environmental equipment on the surface could be used to produce breathable air inside each shelter."

"Pressurized domes?" Kirk asked. "Building them is going to be harder than putting the equipment back in the Conestogas."

"The shelters would not have to be pressurized in any fashion," Spock said, "and would only have to carry their own weight, since the siliconic gel is just slightly heavier than the weight of air."

"What about the siliconic gel polymers on the ground inside the sheltered areas, in the soil?" Kirk asked.

"We break it apart, slow it down, the same way you did in that cannister over there," Spock said. "Plowing the ground would break enough of the polymers apart to slow the advancement for days. We should be able to come up with a simpler, safer way of doing the same thing."

Kirk nodded. From what he was beginning to understand about the siliconic gel, the biggest threat from it—after it was formed—was the fact that it shoved the oxygen away, causing anyone breathing the siliconic gel to suffocate. Siliconic gel itself was basically just silicon and nothing more.

"Am I to understand then that any building closed against the normal elements would serve the same function for the short term?" Kirk asked.

Spock nodded. "As long as the supply of oxygen lasted."

Kirk looked at Scotty and Spock, then nodded. "All right, we attack this from three fronts. Mr. Scott, keep working on those ships. I want as many of them ready to hold people as you can get, as fast as you can get them in shape. Do whatever it takes and keep me informed regularly."

"Aye, Captain."

"Mr. Spock, you keep working on a way to stop the nanoassemblers."

"Understood," Spock said.

"I'm going to talk to the governor about finding shelter for everyone on the planet. He's going to love this."

"Better than goin' back to the ships," Scotty said.

"Maybe," Kirk said. He wasn't convinced, and he doubted Governor Pardonnet was going to be either.

The arid, desert canyon cut across the landscape as if a huge knife had sliced open the face of the planet. The hot wind whipped at Pardonnet's face as he moved to the edge, away from Captain Kirk and Mary, and looked down. The walls were brown rock and vertical, plunging at least two hundred feet down to a canyon floor. A stream ran through the valley from Pardonnet's left to right, and there were trees and brush along the water's edge, forming a green strip down the center.

The siliconic gel clearly hadn't advanced far yet in

the canyon floor, because the plants still seemed very green. Or maybe it was only in comparison with the dry, plantless desert around him that they looked alive.

The opposite canyon rim was a good two hundred meters across, and the canyon seemed to run straight for kilometers in both directions, as if someone had actually measured it and built it. A dozen of his engineers were working the other side of the canyon, taking readings, preparing for what was to come.

"Well, Captain," Pardonnet said, "think we can cover most of this?"

Kirk nodded, turning his back on the wind to face Pardonnet. "Possible. This is a better situation than I had hoped you'd find."

"Actually," Pardonnet said, glancing back at the canyon, "I didn't know this was even here. Mary told me about it after she heard your idea about staying on the surface."

"Made a day trip here last month," Mary said. "Thought it was interesting."

"It is," Kirk said, smiling at her.

"My engineers think we can have it covered quickly," Pardonnet said. "Two or three days to cover a full kilometer of canyon. And we'll keep adding more each day. It should fit the entire colony population easily in a week or so."

"How about securing it against storms?"

Pardonnet smiled. He liked being ahead of Kirk once in a while, especially on important things like this. "Already thought about that, Captain. My people say that won't be a problem. We'll even build a temporary dam and water diversion system upstream in case of a sudden flood."

"Good thinking," Kirk said. "Evacuate all your personnel from the danger areas first, get them here working. But keep your scientists trying to find a solution to the siliconic gel."

Pardonnet laughed. "Don't worry, Captain. I'm shoving them every hour on the hour." And he had been. The Starfleet scientists were good, but he also trusted his people more. If there was a solution to be found, and he knew there was, his scientists would find it.

Kirk nodded and leaned over the edge, looking down. "How about digging rooms into the sides of the cliff faces?" He glanced back at Pardonnet. "That going to be possible?"

Pardonnet moved up beside the captain, staring at the almost smooth walls of the canyon on the opposite side. Again he was ahead of Kirk. "More than possible, Captain. In fact, the rock structure allows easy digging and needs very little support blocking. All private living areas will be in the walls, all public buildings will be along the valley floor."

"You're going to need to plow up that soil," Kirk said, pointing at the trees and brush.

"Even better," Pardonnet said. "The soil along the bottom is only a thin layer. We're going to move it all out, scrape the entire area under the covering down to rock before we start, to make sure we're safe. Assuming the nanoassemblers don't use rock as I have been told they don't."

"They don't," Kirk said. "And without the soil the entire place will be cleaner as well."

"Exactly," Pardonnet said. "We'll drill for water and everyone will go on food rations."

"How long can you last here?"

Pardonnet glanced at Mary. He'd had her roughly figure out the answer to that very question the hour before. He indicated she should give the answer to Kirk.

"We should have enough supplies to make it at least three months if needed," Mary said.

"Let's hope it's not needed," Kirk said, clearly not happy with the answer. "But that at least buys us all some time. We'll find a solution. If the Kauld can build it, we can tear it apart."

"The problem is," Pardonnet said, "it doesn't buy the planet much time. Right?"

Kirk nodded again, but said nothing.

Pardonnet knew that if they didn't find a solution in a matter of a week or two at the outside, staying on Belle Terre was going to be a moot point. There wouldn't be an animal, insect, or tree left alive on the planet. And in that case, Belle Terre certainly wouldn't be a place to have a colony.

Pardonnet stared at the rock canyon below him. Living in caves in a covered canyon was a long way from what he had envisioned his colony to be when he left Earth. But they were going to do what they had to do to survive. And if it meant living in caves, then all of them would live in caves.

Chapter Six

TEGAN WELCH sat beside Charles's bed, holding his hand, watching the other patients' family members come and go from the ward. None of the five sick patients seemed to be getting any better. Charles had had a rough night's sleep and Dr. Akins decided it was better for all of them to stay mostly sedated. He swore to Tegan that twenty-four hours was far too soon to tell if there was going to be any improvement.

She didn't believe him for a moment.

Since the decision to start evacuating the dangerous areas on the planet, all the other patients' families had moved to the hospital ship as well. And all the Starfleet personnel had returned to stay. But even then, the ship still seemed abandoned. On a ship designed to hold hundreds and hundreds, forty to fifty people just didn't seem like many. And except in the medical ward, with the patients, Tegan didn't usually see any of the ship's crew, even when she was out exploring.

She still hadn't had a chance to talk to Captain Skaerbaek alone, although he had stopped by the ward once to see how everyone was doing. He had looked busy and worried, but she didn't ask him why. She just figured that her idea of taking one of the hospital ship's shuttles was her best plan at the moment, so she focused on it. Trying to get his help to leave the system was just going to have to wait.

Every hour she would leave Charles and wander down near the shuttlebay, hoping to accidentally meet a crewman. It was on her fourth such walk that she had success. Just beyond the entrance to the shuttlebay a young woman worked on a panel. She was clearly part of the engineering staff. She had dark blond hair and looked to be around thirty, Tegan's age.

"Hi," Tegan said, stopping a few feet from the crew member.

The woman turned and a smile lit up her faceful of freckles. "Tegan Welch, correct?" the woman said.

Tegan was taken back. "Right. How'd you know?"

The woman laughed, a high, infectious laugh that she must have used often. "You're not crew, so you must be family, and the only family your age on board is named Tegan Welch." She smiled and extended a hand. "I'm Ensign Bonnie Harrow."

Tegan shook the firm hand of Bonnie Harrow, then laughed as well. "I'm impressed you took the time to learn the passengers' names."

"Captain Skaerbaek makes it a priority to know the

passengers, and have his crew know them as much as possible," Ensign Harrow said. "I've been with the ship now for three years. It's become a habit."

"And a good one," Tegan said.

"How's your son?" Harrow asked. "Any improvement?"

Tegan shook her head. "Still the same, I'm afraid. But Dr. Akins says it's too early yet to expect changes."

Harrow nodded. "Still doesn't keep you from being disappointed, though."

"You got that right," Tegan said. Then she glanced back at the door. If she could now just get the ensign to take her in there. "I saw the other day you have two shuttles."

"Yup," Harrow said, finishing something inside the panel and closing it. *"Little Brother* and *Little Sister.* Nice little ships."

"You fly them?" Tegan asked.

Harrow nodded. "Sure do. All of us regular Starfleet who came along on this mission had to know how to pilot the shuttles. Just in case of emergencies."

"That makes sense," Tegan said. This next bit was going to either get her in one of the shuttles or make this entire conversation a waste of time. "I sure miss flying shuttles. Did a training stint on Earth for six months before we set off. Loved it."

"You've flown shuttles, huh?" Harrow said, smiling. "Bet you'd love to see the insides of one of these then."

Tegan laughed. "I thought you'd never offer."

Tegan couldn't believe her luck. Her plan had worked. Harrow gave her the full tour of *Little Sister,* right down to letting her sit in the pilot's chair and run through the controls. As Tegan had figured, she could fly it. In fact, it wasn't that different from the one she had trained on.

And knowing that made her feel a lot better.

She agreed to meet Ensign Harrow later for a late lunch, then headed back to the ward to sit with Charles. All the way she smiled. Step two complete. Now she just had to wait for the right moment. And the way she figured it, that moment was at least fourteen hours away, during the next Gamma Night. And she had a lot to do between now and then.

Captain Kirk stared at the image of the tiny Kauld nanoassembler that filled the small screen in the makeshift science lab. It was hard for him to believe that the square-looking machine was so small that thousands of them could fit on the head of a pin. And that each one was a tiny factory that rebuilt more factories just like it, as well as building siliconic gel polymers.

He knew that nanomachines of different sorts and complexities had been around on Earth since the late twentieth century, but they still fascinated him. And worried him at the same time. He could fight something big and powerful. That he was used to. But fighting machines that were too small to even be seen, and that built new machines just like themselves, was hard for him to grasp. It was why Earth governments for centuries had severely limited and regulated the use of nanomachines.

"So, Mr. Spock," Kirk said, turning from the screen.

"Now that we know what we're dealing with, how do we stop them?"

"I do not know, Captain," Spock said.

"Have you tried chemicals?" Kirk asked. He figured that since the things looked like little bugs, and acted much like a virus, maybe chemicals would kill them.

"I have done one hundred and six logical tests of different compounds," Spock said. "No results."

"Electrical charges?" Kirk asked.

"A strong enough charge does shut down the nanoassemblers," Spock said, staring at the captain.

Kirk suddenly saw the wound across Spock's forehead and remembered that Spock had destroyed the science lab by putting an electical charge into the soil. "Never mind," Kirk said, waving his hand. "How about sonic?"

"A high level of sonic vibration does break apart the siliconic gel molecules, but does not shut down the nanoassemblers or their ability to produce the polymers. I have reported my discovery to the team on the planet."

"Good," Kirk said. "Might help them fight back the siliconic gel in certain places that need protection."

"That, yes," Spock said, "but I suggested they set up sonic defenders aimed into the sky on all sides of the canyon city they are building, to keep oxygen-rich atmosphere flowing from above the levels of the siliconic gel down and into the city. They agreed it would be a good idea."

Kirk just shook his head. Amazing what they were having to come up with to escape this Kauld attack. But he still believed that if the Kauld could build something like that tiny machine on the screen, Spock and the colonist scientists could find a way to stop it.

Then he realized what he had been missing. "Spock, we need a fourth front of attack at this problem."

"And what might that be, Captain?" Spock said, his eyebrow arching as it always did when trying to follow human logic.

"We missed one of the basic rules of solving a problem. We need to go to the source to find our solution."

"Captain," Spock said, "the source is the Kauld."

"Exactly," Kirk said. "And since they attacked us, I doubt if they're going to just give us the solution, do you?"

"Highly unlikely, Captain," Spock said.

"So then," Kirk said, smiling at his first officer. "I guess we're just going to have to go and take the answer from them."

Spock just stared at his smile, but did not object.

Lilian Coates stared out the window at the canyon that was to be her new home as the transport swooped in toward the unloading sight. It was going to be almost everyone on Belle Terre's new home, if the siliconic gel wasn't stopped soon. The canyon and desert around it seemed barren and stark compared with the almost tropical island she had just left. The canyon itself looked like a slice in the ground and was nothing but rock and a running stream down the middle.

The entire bottom of the canyon, for as far as she could see in both directions, had been scraped clear down to the stone, leaving the stream muddy and still finding its new channel. In a dozen places crews were working to install beams that extended in an arch over the canyon. She had been told those support beams would hold a double layer of a special rubber membrane to hold out the siliconic gel and the atmosphere inside. They were producing the membrane in a small, quickly built plant about a hundred paces from the canyon rim.

She could also see against the far wall drillers hollowing out rooms from the side of the cliffs, cutting staircases and ramps, and building living places. The extra rock pulled from the walls was being formed into walkways and buildings on the canyon floor. Entire log structures had also been airlifted in and placed on the canyon floor, including Governor Pardonnet's office. Almost before her eyes a town was being born. It was amazing what necessity could do.

And how fast it could be done.

The transport touched down without even a bump and a few moments later she was helping the ground crew unload the school supplies and machines she and Reynold and a few others had carefully packed. There was still a little more to get, but not much. For some reason, having the school machines and library disks all in a safe place made her feel much, much better.

Reynold and their cat were already here at the canyon. Reynold was with a hundred other schoolchildren of his age, being taken care of in a building a half mile from the canyon construction. She had set that up first thing after Gamma Night cleared, so the parents of all the children would have the time to keep working, knowing their children were safe.

Not having to worry about Reynold had certainly freed her time as well.

It took less than five minutes before everything was unloaded from the transport and headed for its assigned location in the canyon.

She climbed back into the passenger seat of the transport and nodded to the pilot that she was ready. With surge and twist, they were airborne, headed back toward the large island she had called home.

It still was her home. She refused to think any other way. They were just moving for a short time, and would soon be back, she was sure.

The flight time was less than ten minutes, and during that time she worked over what was left to be done. She had to get her and Reynold's things from her home and get them to the transport pad. Thank heavens Reynold had insisted on taking the cat with him to the canyon location. That was one worry missing now.

She also had to finish getting the rest of the school equipment and supplies to the transport. That would come first, then her own things. After that she was finished, and her work could start on the other side, setting up the new school, unpacking the supplies she had just spent hours packing.

As they swept in toward the island, a dark weather front was looming to the west and slightly north. The clouds were not something she had wanted to see. With luck, the transports wouldn't be grounded if the storm came ashore. Or better yet, maybe they would get lucky and the storm would hold off until they were done.

The transport settled on to the pad and she jumped out as the crew there started loading the next equipment and baggage to go to the canyon. There were only about twenty people left around the transport area, and she could tell that half of them at least would go with this ride. What had once been the main colony town was becoming a ghost town. She had been through this once before, only then she had had no intention of leaving. This time she had every intention of leaving, and leaving as soon as she was done with this last load. She had no desire, as they say, of being the one to turn out the lights.

The storm on the horizon, from the ground, looked even more threatening than it did from the air. She waited until the transport was loaded; then, at a fast walk, she and two of the crew helping load the transport headed for the old school building to get the last of the equipment and supplies. By the time they got it back to the platform, the second transport was coming in for a landing. Perfect timing.

She made sure it all got loaded, then headed up the gravel road. A quick trip up to her home to get her and Reynold's luggage and a few pictures, and then she would be on the following flight to safety.

As she headed up her sidewalk, she was amazed at how bad her garden looked. It hadn't been that long, but it seemed the Kauld machines in the soil were really doing their jobs. She had spent a lot of hours in that garden. It made her mad to have to leave it and her home.

Inside she did a quick walk-through to make sure she

hadn't left anything. She didn't want to dwell here too long. It would be too hard having to leave if she did that. It was hard enough as it was. Better to do this quickly and get out. She had no doubt she'd be back very soon.

She had just started to pick up the last of the suitcases when a rumbling shook the air, like a distant thunder, followed by a shock wave that tumbled her over backward.

The rumbling grew.

It was clearly an earthquake, getting louder and louder as everything around her shook. Then slowly it faded and the silence came back. The silence seemed almost as unnatural as the rumbling and shaking.

She staggered to her feet, grabbed the suitcases again, and was about to make a run for the transport pad when another distant rumble filled the air, again followed by a massive earthquake that again knocked her down and shook her house the way a child would shake a toy.

Dust and debris flew everywhere, and a cupboard smashed off the wall to the ground.

She held on to the edge of the kitchen counter and waited, forcing herself to stay calm.

This time when the rumbling stopped, she stayed down long enough to wait for another wave. Long seconds of deep, intense silence as her breathing seemed to fill every ounce of her awareness. For the moment it seemed as if another wasn't coming. But if those were earthquakes, there was sure to be aftershocks. She wanted to be on the transport and headed for the canyon when they came.

The air around her was swirling with dust, and the

light from the windows looked tainted with orange and red. She had scraped her knee and jammed a finger when she fell, but otherwise she was all right.

She gathered the luggage one more time and headed for the door. She had no idea what was happening, but whatever it was, it couldn't be good. She had heard rumors that the siliconic gel could be explosive. She just wished she had listened more closely when they were talking about that.

She pulled the door open and was instantly smacked by something that felt like a spiderweb.

It seemed to cover her, choke her breath, stick to her eyes, as if she had walked into a thousand spiderwebs, sticky and deadly.

She screamed and the web-feel filled her mouth, wrapped around her tongue, choked at her.

She managed to pull back and slam the door closed.

Then staggering, she moved back into the living room, clawing at her face, coughing the feeling of webs out of her mouth. She managed to catch her breath and the web feeling quickly vanished from her skin, leaving only the sensation of something crawling on her.

She brushed her arms and just stood in the middle of her living room, shuddering.

After a few more deep breaths, she moved to the window and looked out down the street. It was as if she were staring through a thin layer of water instead of air. Everything looked just slightly blurry.

Siliconic gel.

That was the only thing it could be.

The entire area was suddenly covered with siliconic

gel. Now she knew what siliconic gel felt like and she didn't like it at all.

A body lay on the street a hundred meters below her house. She couldn't tell who it was, but it was clearly not moving. More than likely the person had suffocated trying to breathe in the siliconic gel as she had tried to do. She didn't want to think about what the transport pad might hold.

She turned back to stare at her small home. At the moment, the walls and windows were the only things keeping her safe from the siliconic gel surrounding her. And she had no idea how long that would last. Or how long her breathable air would last.

She was in a cave again, just as in the last evacuation. Only this time, the cave was her own home and for the moment Reynold was safe. At least that much she could be thankful for.

She just had no idea how to get out. Or if she ever would.

Chapter Seven

KIRK WAS STUDYING a recent Kauld movement report from the two scout ships he had patrolling the system. It seemed the Kauld were keeping their distance at the moment, a detail that would not be unusual in and of itself, but combined with the attack by their nanoassemblers, it made sense. They had no need to get close, except to watch. Somewhere, one of the Kauld ships, or outpost, had to be watching. Kirk knew them well enough to know that. He just had to find them. And then get the information from them on how to stop their nasty little machines.

"Captain," Lieutenant Uhura's voice said, clearly full of worry. "We've got a problem on the main island."

He glanced around at her and instantly knew something was very, very wrong. He'd watched Uhura's expressions for years and could read her like a book.

"What happened?"

"A lightning storm triggered some explosions," she said. "Not everyone was off the island yet. There are thirty-seven missing."

"Lilian?" Kirk asked, already knowing the answer from Uhura's face.

"I'm afraid so," Uhura said.

"Any contact with anyone from the island at all?"

Uhura shook her head.

"Put a visual on screen," he said.

A moment later the main string of colony islands appeared. A large storm system was swirling to the east and north of the main island, just brushing the land.

"Increase magnification," Kirk said. "Focus on the main colony site. Scan for life."

The island chain vanished and the screen was filled with the images of the colony. Everything looked fuzzy and out of focus. His stomach twisted as he realized what he was seeing. "I assume that's the best image," Kirk said. "Nothing wrong with the equipment."

Uhura nodded. "Something seems to be blocking the visuals of the ground. And scanning is also blocked."

"Siliconic gel," Kirk said. "A very thick layer of it, from the looks of it. Pull back just slightly. I want to be able to see the entire island."

It was clear at once where the leading edge of the siliconic gel was, from the distortion in the view. And the siliconic gel cloud was moving fast toward the lower side of the island. Luckily there was no one there. Everyone had been up in the center of the island, at the main town area.

"Is there any way to tell if anyone is alive down there?"

Uhura shook her head no. "I've been trying, but the distortion is just too great."

"Which means we can't beam in there either," Kirk said, more to himself.

He stared at the island. He knew that anyone inside during the wave of siliconic gel coming over might still be alive. The siliconic gel wasn't poisonous in and of itself. It simply suffocated its victims by forcing all the air away. However, any air inside a house would also remain in the house for the same reason. The siliconic gel wouldn't hold it there, but it also wouldn't push it out very quickly. It would be more like a bubble trapped in a space under water. It would last for a short time, then slowly leak away upward, since the siliconic gel was heavier then breathable atmosphere. If anyone alive down there had a chance, they were going to have to be rescued quickly.

"Have Dr. McCoy meet us in the shuttlebay. And have full suits ready."

"Yes, sir," Uhura said.

"And tell Governor Pardonnet that we're going into the area, and to keep his people out."

"Understood," Uhura said.

"Mr. Sulu, you're with me."

Kirk knew that flying onto an island covered with siliconic gel would be risky, at best, but if anyone was left alive down there, going in was the only way to get them out. He didn't want to think about how he would find Lilian. But if she was still alive, he was going to try to get there in time.

Kirk and Sulu were already climbing into their suits when McCoy reached the shuttlebay.

"Jim, are you nuts?" McCoy asked. "That place is going to be like flying into the middle of an exploding volcano."

Sulu smiled. "After flying around the Big Muddy through all those olivium storms, Doc, an exploding volcano's going to be like a vacation."

"Besides, Bones, the siliconic gel in and of itself isn't explosive."

McCoy snorted. "That storm is setting off explosion after explosion, Jim. You saw what being in one of those explosions did to Spock."

"I know the risks, Bones, but if there are survivors, we've got to find them." Kirk finished with his suit and climbed aboard the shuttle. Sulu was right behind him. "Finish getting in your suit on the way down, Doctor," Kirk said. "We're fighting time here."

McCoy just shook his head as he tossed the suit on board ahead of him.

Lilian Coates wasn't sure if her imagination was feeling the siliconic gel again, or if it was really coming inside. It felt as if she were walking against an ankle-high wind, as if the air itself was thicker from just below her knees down to the floor.

She finally forced herself to reach down and sweep her hand just above the floor.

She pulled back instantly, shudders running down her spine like a cold drip of water.

It felt as if her hand were pushing through spider-webs, only without the stickiness.

She shivered again.

"Stop thinking about it," she said out loud, scolding herself, letting the sound of her own voice in her own home calm her nerves. "Do the logical thing to save yourself. Help will be here soon."

She glanced around, then ignoring how it felt to walk through the layer of siliconic gel, she moved across the living room, pulled open the blinds so she could see down the road toward the main village, and then sat on the couch with her feet up. When the siliconic gel reached the level of the couch, then she'd worry about finding a place higher up. But for the moment, she could see anyone coming up the road, and they should be able to see her.

The body on the road was that of a woman. From the angle of the front window she could tell that now. But she still couldn't tell which of her neighbors it was.

This was so strange. She was just sitting on her couch, looking out her front window as she had done so many times in the past. Outside looked almost normal, except for the weird fuzziness to the air, as if the window had been melted slightly.

And the body in the road.

Yet she knew that her house was worse than being under water at the moment. In siliconic gel, there was no swimming up to reach the surface and safety. She was trapped on the bottom, and if she lost her air bubble inside the house, she would die just as surely as a swimmer drowning.

Drowning in spiderwebs.

Again she shuddered.

"Stop thinking about it!" she said aloud. Hearing her own voice helped.

There was another distant thunder rumble and then again the ground shook. On the couch it didn't feel as strong as the first two, but the house and windows all shook. She held her breath, hoping she wouldn't hear the sound of glass breaking. If she did she'd take a deep breath and try to make a run for the main building down the hill.

After a moment the rumbling stopped and again everything was quiet.

Deathly quiet.

She eased her hand down over the edge of the couch slightly. The level of siliconic gel was halfway up. It wouldn't be long until she would be sitting in it, and would have to move.

She looked around the one-story home she had helped build. Where was she going to move to? That was the question.

Over her head open beams stretched across the room. If she had to, she'd climb up there. But she had no intention of dying up there. She'd try to make a run for it if the siliconic gel got up there as well.

Otherwise, she was just going to stay put and hope for rescue. By now Jim would know she was in trouble. And having the most famous starship captain in the Federation working to save her made her feel better.

A distant thunder, followed by a hard earthquake that again shook the room.

This one felt closer and more intense. But again, no windows broke and she let out the breath she had been holding.

It seemed in this situation, she was going to be holding her breath a lot.

Governor Pardonnet stared at the images coming in over his monitor from a ship relay. The thunder storm to the north of the main colony's island was causing havoc. Every time a lightning strike hit the ground, there was a massive explosion that sent plumes of soil and rock hundreds of feet into the air.

He knew what that explosion was. Siliconic gel, being formed instantly from polymers created in the soil by the nanoassemblers. The earthquakes were being felt from the explosions a hundred kilometers away. Who knew what the quakes were doing to the buildings and materials left in the main colony. And the poor people still there.

He doubted anyone could still be alive. The siliconic gel had covered the entire town to a level of fifty feet deep almost instantly. It was blurring all sensors and vision. Kirk was taking a shuttle in to see if they could find survivors, but from the images coming in, the chances of anyone being alive in that area were next to none. If the siliconic gel hadn't gotten them, the earthquakes and explosions soon would.

He stepped away from the monitor and stared out down the desert canyon and the construction madly taking place on the floor, in the walls, and overhead. This place was going to have to survive with the same level of destruction and earthquakes the first time a storm came through here. Luckily, this was a desert area, and storms were rare here. But the siliconic gel would still cover them soon enough if they didn't find a way to stop it.

Could this canyon survive a pounding like the one the island was taking right now? He'd have to make sure the engineers saw these images and then ask them that same question.

Maybe, just maybe, he should be focusing his efforts on getting back to the ships, getting them ready to go again. He knew Kirk had a number of crews on the Conestogas doing just that. Maybe Kirk was right. Belle Terre, from the looks of those images coming over the screen, was going to be a dead planet very soon. He just didn't want it taking too many of the colonists with it to the grave.

Chapter Eight

SULU BROUGHT the shuttle in smoothly near the colony transport pad. Kirk couldn't believe the strangeness of it. At a hundred feet the atmosphere was clear, at fifty feet it was thick and rough. Outside the shuttle the town looked, at first glance, to be in good shape. It was only on closer inspection, through the shimmering of the siliconic gel, that it became clear the earthquakes were taking their toll. A roof of one building had slid sideways, and two walls of another structure had completely collapsed.

A colony transport was on the pad, its cargo bay doors open. Two bodies were sprawled near it and Kirk could see another body at the controls and a few others in the passenger seats. If the transport had been locked up, ready to take off, the pilot and passengers would have made it out alive. As it was, they died in their seats, fighting for air that wasn't there.

He let his gaze drift up the hill toward Lilian's house. How many times had he walked that hill on a warm evening? He pushed the thought back and moved to get ready to go out.

"Jim," McCoy said, pointing through the window of the shuttle. "They're alive in the transport."

"What?" He spun to look back at the colony ship. The pilot, a young-looking man with a mask over his face, was waving weakly at them.

"Let's get over there," Kirk said.

Moving as fast as they dared, they went through the shuttle airlock and out into the thick-feeling air. Kirk corrected his thinking. It wasn't actually air, Kirk knew. It was siliconic gel, a silicone substance, yet it looked like air. You just couldn't breathe it. It would be like trying to breathe sand or glass.

The transport pilot and the four passengers were all alive, but barely. All had masks on their faces and terrified looks in their eyes. Kirk had never seen four people so happy to see him. He just wished one of them had been Lilian. But no such luck.

Sulu moved up next to the pilot and adjusted the comm link on the transport's control board so that they could talk to the pilot on the same frequency as their suits. McCoy set about checking each of the passengers one at a time.

"Are you all right?" Kirk asked, moving up and kneeling beside the pilot's chair while Spock moved into the copilot's position.

"Been better," the pilot said, his voice barely holding back on breaking. "The stuff feels like spiders crawling on your skin."

Kirk shuddered at that thought. He'd never been much of a fan of spiders.

"Oh, wonderful," McCoy said under his breath. "Remind me to never take this suit off."

"I was afraid to fire up the transport and take off for fear of an explosion. And we didn't have enough oxygen to last much longer. We're glad you got here in time."

Kirk nodded. "We're glad we got here, too. What's your name?"

"Benny, sir," the pilot said.

"Benny, did you see anyone else alive?"

"When the first earthquake hit, and this stuff covered us, a few people ran for the big building there. They made it inside, but I haven't seen any movement since."

"Thanks," Kirk said.

"Can the transport fly?" Sulu asked.

"It could when I landed," the pilot said. "We've been taking some pretty good shaking, but these babies are pretty rugged."

"Are you able to fly it?" Kirk asked.

The pilot squared his shoulders, took a deep breath off his mask, and nodded. "I can do it."

"Jim," McCoy said, "these people are going to be all right. Shock and a slight lack of oxygen is all."

"I had the air turned as low as I dared for all of us," the pilot said. "To give us more time."

Kirk patted him on the shoulder. "You did great, Benny. Give us a minute to get out and button you up, then head for the canyon settlement. I want the doctors there to check you all over. Understood?"

"Won't I cause an explosion?" the pilot asked, his eyes wide with worry.

"The explosions are caused by an electrical charge," Kirk said. "If you've been landing and taking off for the last day without causing one, you won't cause one now. It's the polymers that create the siliconic gel that explode, not the siliconic gel itself."

The pilot nodded, clearly not convinced, but willing to take the chance if Kirk said it was all right.

"Just get the transport quickly up over two hundred feet and you'll be fine," Kirk said to the young man. "Air the cockpit out up there."

"Understood, sir," the pilot said.

They all climbed out and Sulu sealed the transport door.

"All right, Benny," Kirk said. "Take her up nice and slow, just like you've always done."

"Never been one for slow, sir," Benny said. "But I'll try."

McCoy laughed. "He sounds like you when you were younger, Jim."

"What's that, sir?" Benny said.

"Nothing," Kirk said, shaking his head at McCoy. "Just get yourself and your passengers safely to the canyon."

"Copy that. Here goes."

The transport rumbled to life and after a moment lifted off slowly, heading straight up. After a moment Benny's voice came back happy and strong. "We're in clear air up here and it feels wonderful!! Thanks."

"You are more than welcome," Kirk said. He then pointed to the large town hall building, and without another word the three of them headed there. So far their mission had saved five lives. Kirk just hoped Lilian's life would be number six.

The siliconic gel had finally reached the level of the chairs and couch during the last earthquake, so Lilian had waded through it, ignoring the sensations on her legs, and climbed on the kitchen countertop. She could sit there for a while; when the siliconic gel got even higher, she could climb up in the rafters next.

So far she hadn't allowed herself to think of not being rescued. She knew both Pardonnet and Jim wouldn't allow people here to just die. It was just a matter of holding on long enough for the rescue to arrive.

A low rumble filled the room and she braced for another earthquake. But this time there wasn't one. In fact, the rumble sounded different than the distant thunder. More like a transport taking off.

Or landing.

She dropped down off the counter into the siliconic gel and waded to the front window, the resistance against her legs light, yet very present. She could see the main buildings, but not the transport pad. If they were landing there, she wouldn't be able to see them.

For an instant she thought she saw a figure in a spacesuit go inside the large building, but she wasn't sure.

She desperately wanted to go back and crawl up on the counter, but instead forced herself to remain standing in front of the window. If there was someone down there, she needed them to see her.

Around her knees the siliconic gel moved slowly, as if alive with a thousand spiders crawling on her.

On the streets nothing moved at all.

Kirk wasn't sure if the resistance to walking was from the spacesuit, or the siliconic gel around him. It felt almost as if he were moving in a very thin, very clear water, only without any bouyancy at all. Knowing that the siliconic gel was made of mostly silicon didn't help him at all. He didn't want to think about moving around inside glass.

They forced the door to the large meeting hall open and went inside. The light was weak through the windows and shadows filled the corners and upper areas. At first Kirk couldn't see anyone, or any bodies.

"Up here!"

"You hear that?" McCoy said, pointing his flashlight beam up into the rafters. High above them in the large building, ten people clung for their lives on the wooden beams.

"Hurry!" one of them shouted. "It's almost to us."

"Our air is leaking out the roof!" another one shouted.

Kirk immediately reached into his backpack for the air masks with their own short supply of oxygen. He, McCoy, and Sulu each were carrying ten, and there were more in the shuttle if they needed them. The masks would last ten minutes, enough oxygen for the people to climb down and get into the shuttle. But somehow they had to get the masks up to the people first, and that was going to be a problem in the suits. Spacesuits were just not made for climbing in normal gravity.

"Any ideas?" Kirk asked.

Neither McCoy nor Sulu said a word as they looked up.

"All right, then," Kirk said. "I'm going to take this suit off and use a mask myself."

"Jim," McCoy said, "I wouldn't recommend that—"

Too late. He had released the latches on his helmet and taken it off, grabbing an oxygen mask as he did and covering his mouth.

The pilot had been right. The siliconic gel felt like spiders crawling over his face and down his neck. He wanted to instantly start swatting at them, even though he knew they weren't there. He hated spiders.

And it felt as if they were on his face, his neck, his arms. Crawling down his back.

He secured the mask over his face and quickly got rid of the rest of his suit, ignoring the feel of spiderwebs all over his body and pressing against his clothes. In all his years, this was the worst thing he had ever felt.

He forced himself to breathe slowly to save the oxygen in his mask, then slung the backpack over his shoulder and looked for the best way up.

"Stairs in the back will get you to the next level," a voice shouted down from the rafters.

"Please hurry!" another shouted.

Kirk waved that he had heard, then moved off, indicating that McCoy and Sulu should follow as best they could.

Walking in the siliconic gel without a suit wasn't much easier than in a suit. And it felt very, very odd, as if he were constantly pushing through webs. It was just enough resistance to be very noticeable, but not enough to really stop him.

He forced his way up the stairs and to a ladder on the wall that led up into the rafters.

Ten minutes later he was handing masks to very happy colonists sitting on beams, and then helping them climb down.

Ten minutes after that all ten survivors were in the shuttle being checked over by Dr. McCoy.

Fifteen survivors so far, and Lilian Coates was not among them.

Chapter Nine

LILIAN COATES stood at her front window, staring down the road as the rain started, making the siliconic gel shimmer as the water ran through it, pelting the ground not so much in drops, but in a mist. And if the rain was here, so was the lightning that was triggering the explosions.

She wanted to move back from the window to a place a little safer, to a place where she didn't have to stand in waist-deep siliconic gel, but she also knew she didn't dare. If there was a rescue mission going on, she needed to be seen. So for the moment she was going to stay near the window.

The siliconic gel seemed to be breaking the raindrops apart as they fell, forming thousands of colors seemingly in midair. Shimmering, tiny rainbows that under different circumstances would have been beautiful. At the moment it was just making her more scared, making it clear to her that what was surrounding her home was something very different than normal air.

She could feel it around her legs as well, and imagine the bubble of oxygen she was breathing getting smaller and smaller.

She pushed the thought away and stared down the gravel road, between the trees and buildings. Twice in the last few minutes she had been convinced she saw movement down near the main meeting hall, but the trees and other homes along the road blocked most of her line of sight.

She guessed that it was at least a hundred and fifty running paces down that hill before she could get the transport area in sight, and another good hundred running paces more before she would reach that. Could she run two hundred and fifty steps, in siliconic gel, on one breath?

She wasn't sure she could. She had never been very good at holding her breath, and just twenty running steps usually winded her. But if she had to do it to save her life, she was going to try.

For a few moments it looked as if the rain was going to ease up some. Then suddenly there was a sharp crack as a bolt of lightning smashed into the ground up the hill somewhere behind her home.

The next instant it felt as if the entire house was jerked upward and then smashed back down again.

She was tossed into the air with the furniture, and then back and away from the window. She tumbled against the couch and her favorite end table snapped down over her. Instantly her face and hands were completely covered in the spiderweb-like feeling of the siliconic gel.

Her first response was to scream, but she stopped that, forcing herself to not breathe at all. Instead she just held on to the edge of the couch.

The rumbling continued and the house shook. The noise was louder than she could have imagined possible, shaking her viciously. She realized that part of the noise she was hearing was smashing glass.

Some of her windows were breaking.

Again she forced herself to not scream.

She kept what little breath she had, biting her lip to keep her mouth closed and using one hand to hold her nose like she was about to jump in a pool. The siliconic gel web-feel covered her face, her neck, her hands. She knew it was impossible to wipe away, but her first instinct was to do just that.

Quickly, as the shaking lessened, she scrambled to her feet and across the jumble of what had once been her furniture.

She reached the kitchen counter and climbed up on it as quickly as she could, then reached above for the wooden joists that ran across the kitchen and helped support the roof. She could reach them fairly easily. She pulled hard on one to test if it would hold her. It still felt fairly solid.

She used the last of her strength to pull herself up, swinging one leg over and then twisting her body on top of the beam so that she rested on the top, with the rough wood between her breasts. She felt her face clear the siliconic gel and the feeling of spiderwebs.

For the moment she was above it.

She took a gasping breath and let herself remain facedown on the narrow beam, holding on to it with a grip so tight that splinters cut her hands. The pain of the splinters didn't matter, as long as she could breathe.

Another, smaller explosion and earthquake threatened to dump her from the beam, but she managed to ride it out like a child hanging on to a play horse.

When it stopped she took more deep breaths, then reached her hand down toward the counter. Not more than a foot below her she could feel the spiderweb-feel of the siliconic gel rising toward her. The earthquake must have broken some holes or cracks in the roof as well as the windows, and her air was leaking slowly out above her.

She didn't have much time left. She was going to have to figure out a plan and do it fast.

Below her it looked as if a bar fight had occurred in her living room. Broken furniture and glass were everywhere, and one of her suitcases had broken open, scattering her clothes.

She forced herself to take a deep breath, then another, then another, doing her best to calm down, if that was possible while hanging on to a wooden beam for dear life.

"Think, Lilian!" she said out loud. Her voice sounded very contained and didn't make her feel better at all.

It looked as if she was going to have no choice but to make a run for it very soon. And the only way to do that was have two lungs full of good air.

Water dripped through the roof on her back, startling her.

"Calm down, Lilian," she said, aloud, her voice again sounding small and muted in the remaining airspace above her kitchen. "You can do this."

Her hands gripped the beam even tighter. She might be able to do it, but she sure didn't want to.

"Jim, where are you?"

The loud explosion and earthquake rocked the *Enterprise* shuttle as if a mad god were angry at it, spinning it, banging it, then spinning it around again. The ten colonists and the three crew were tossed around inside like rag dolls. Luckily, for all of them, it didn't last long.

Kirk pushed himself up off the floor, where he had ended up braced against a bulkhead, and glanced at McCoy. "You all right?"

McCoy pulled off the helmet to his suit and tossed it aside. "If being inside an old amusement park ride without being belted in properly is all right, I guess I'm fine."

"Sulu?"

"Just fine, Captain," Sulu said, despite the fact that he had sustained a deep cut to the upper arm. Kirk could see the blood coming through the suit.

Sulu immediately moved to check on the condition of the shuttle's systems.

McCoy and Kirk quickly helped the others to get back on their feet as another small quake, nowhere near as severe as the first, struck the shuttle. After it passed, McCoy did a quick check of the survivors while Kirk moved up to help Sulu.

"Will it fly?" Kirk said, moving to sit in the copilot's chair. He'd been banged around a lot in a shuttle over the years, but never like that before. Even crash-landing one hadn't felt that hard.

He looked out at the ruined colony. A number of homes had collapsed. After that earthquake, it was going to be even more unlikely there were any more survivors in any of the colony buildings. He wasn't allowing himself to think about losing Lilian.

"No damage worth mentioning, sir," Sulu said. "We'll be fine."

"Good," Kirk said, staring out at the fifty buildings he could see. "How are we going to search all those buildings?"

"We're not," McCoy said, coming up behind him. "We need to get these survivors out of here now."

Kirk looked up at McCoy's intent face. "Bones, we have accounted for seventeen of the thirty-five people lost here. We're not leaving until we find the other eighteen. The question is how are we going to do it. There are a lot of buildings out there to search, and damn little time to search them."

"I'll help," a woman's voice came from behind Bones. She moved up beside the doctor and brushed the long, gray hair from her face. She had to be sixty if she was a day, and her skin tone was pale. But there was a fire in her blue eyes that Kirk liked.

"I don't think so," McCoy said.

She gave him a soily look. "Give me an oxygen mask and tell me where to search. I don't want to go back out in that stuff, but for my neighbors, I will."

"Yeah, count me in," a man's voice came from the back. Two or three others also volunteered.

"Captain, these people have been through enough," McCoy said. "We need to get them out of here and now. Two have broken bones, two others may have concussions, and all are cut and bruised."

Kirk nodded, then looked at the older woman. "What's your name?"

"Francie Evans," she said.

"It's an honor meeting you, Francie," Kirk said, taking the firm grasp of the woman.

"Just glad to be meeting anyone at the moment," she said, smiling.

Kirk nodded. It was going to take help to find the rest, and they needed to move fast if they were going to find anyone alive. He turned to the control board of the shuttle and clicked on the communications link. "Kirk to Benny. Are you out there, son?"

"Right here, Captain," Benny said.

"How far away are you? And do you have enough fuel to return for some passengers?"

"Take a look out your window, Captain," Benny's voice said, coming back strong.

Kirk glanced to his right as the colony transport did a quick turn and landed expertly right were it had left a few minutes before.

"No one listens anymore, do they?" McCoy said, clearly disgusted.

"We were following your adventure on your suit radios and I knew you were going to need more help when you found the ten survivors, so I turned around.

Sure hate being back in this creepy stuff. But I haven't opened up the doors yet."

"How's your air supply?"

"We got about ten minutes on the shuttle supply," Benny said. "So if you want our help, when I open the doors you're going to need to bring some of those air bottles you were talking about."

Kirk glanced around at McCoy, then smiled.

"Told you that kid reminded me of you," McCoy said, shaking his head in clear disgust.

"All right, Benny," Kirk said, smiling at McCoy. "We're going to be bringing you the wounded to take to the canyon. Any of your passengers want to stay and help search, they are more than welcome."

"All of them do, sir," Benny said. "If I wasn't flying this thing, I'd stay as well."

Kirk nodded. "Great. Let's get going. If anyone is alive out there, they're running out of time."

Ten minutes later Benny lifted off again carrying five of the wounded survivors. The other eleven, plus Sulu, McCoy, and Kirk, were going to spread out and search. Each carried extra oxygen and a communicator to call for help.

Kirk stood and watched for the fifteen seconds it took for the shuttle to clear the area. They all did. As it turned out, those fifteen seconds were very important seconds.

The siliconic gel had finally reached the level of the beam. Lilian Coates forced herself to turn and sit up, taking deep, long breaths for as long as she could. She was almost out of time and she knew it. The siliconic gel was coming up fast and in less than a minute it would be over her head even if she was standing on the beam.

She had to act now.

Taking long, deep breaths, she forced herself to stay calm and get as much oxygen in her lungs as she could possibly get. When she dropped off the beam, she figured she had to run down the hill to one of the bigger buildings. With luck, there would be people down there near the transport pad starting search parties, but without luck, she had to make it into the town meeting hall and up to the second floor at least, all on one lungful of air.

She wasn't sure if she could make it to her garden while holding her breath, let alone that far. But she had to try. Staying here was no longer an option.

After a dozen more deep breaths, she took one large one, filling her cheeks and mouth with as much as she could, then rolled off the beam, swinging down to the countertop below as if she had done the move a hundred times. More splinters cut her hands, but that was much better than the feeling of spiderwebs.

The siliconic gel covered her face and arms and head like a scratchy blanket, trying to creep into her nose and mouth.

She held her nose closed and jumped off the counter, then went out the front door at a run.

The rain had stopped, but everything looked dark. And her eyes didn't want to work that well, acting as if dust was constantly hitting them.

She could feel her natural desire to breathe already pounding at her as she jogged into the street and started down the hill. Running in the siliconic gel was like having weights holding your entire body back. It was possible, but not easy. The siliconic gel just didn't want to let her move fast.

After twenty steps she thought her lungs were going to burst, so to ease a little pressure she did what she used to do as a girl while swimming under water and blew out slightly.

That helped for another ten steps, clearing her nose. But it wasn't enough.

She blew out a little more, but now her lungs were telling her to breathe. She wasn't going to listen just yet.

She shoved hard into the siliconic gel, fighting it, pushing it aside.

Ahead she could see that the roof of the large meeting hall was broken, with a large hole in the side. That wasn't going to have any air trapped in there.

The demand for oxygen was getting worse, so she ran faster, racing against the need for air.

Maybe she should duck into one of these houses, see if there was air trapped in them. That would give her a chance to make it farther.

Then ahead of her she could hear a rumble start up.

For a second she wasn't sure if it was just in her own ears, or another earthquake coming, or a transport. She had to believe it was a transport ahead.

As she went past two of the last buildings on the left she could suddenly see the transport area. There was the *Enterprise* shuttle, and a transport there, just starting to take off.

The transport noise was loud now.

And there were people, standing around watching the shuttle, all with air masks over their faces.

Jim was one of them. She knew his broad shoulders and stance anywhere.

She was still seventy-five paces away.

Seventy-five long, long paces.

Too far for how much air she had left.

But she kept running.

Step. Step. Step, one foot in front of the other.

Step.

Step.

They were all still an impossible distance away.

No one was looking at her.

She finally shouted. "Jim!"

But she didn't have enough air to make it a very loud shout.

The siliconic gel filled her mouth, choked her like a ball of cotton jammed down her throat and into her nose.

Run! Keep running!

She couldn't.

She dropped to her knees, coughing, spitting, trying to will herself to not take in any of the siliconic gel, but her body had ideas of its own.

She had to breathe.

She couldn't let herself.

She had to breathe.

She had to!

She opened her mouth and took a deep, gulping breath. But it was more of the siliconic gel instead of oxygen and the silicon substance filled her lungs and nose and throat.

She choked and dropped flat on the ground.

Around her the blackness rushed in, blocking out the light of the day.

She couldn't go like this. Jim was close.

She had to get to him.

Fight! Fight!

With one final bit of energy, she pushed herself to her knees and tried to move toward where Jim stood.

He still wasn't looking at her. His back was turned.

She no longer had any fight left in her.

The blackness took her completely and she didn't even feel the gravel of the road smash into her face.

Chapter Ten

"JIM!"

McCoy's muffled shout through his spacesuit spun Kirk around. He followed where McCoy was pointing and turned just in time to see Lilian fall face-first onto the road and lie there.

At a run he headed for her. Fighting the thickness of the siliconic gel felt almost like running in a swimming pool. It seemed to take forever to reach her, and the entire time he didn't take his gaze from her.

The entire time she didn't move.

It seemed like an eternity before he reached her. He knelt beside her and rolled her over. Her skin was pasty white and blood was seeping from cuts on her checks and forehead.

He quickly slipped an oxygen mask over her face and checked for a pulse. There wasn't one.

He started CPR, but McCoy pushed him aside when he finally lumbered up. "Won't work. She has the siliconic gel in her lungs. Need to get her to the shuttle at once."

All Kirk could do was nod. If there was no oxygen getting to her blood because her lungs were clogged, there was no need to pump the blood. He picked her up in his arms like a child and headed at a slow jog toward the shuttle.

Under normal conditions, he might have struggled with the extra weight, but at this point he didn't notice. He just kept glancing at her face against his shoulder.

McCoy somehow managed to stay at his side, even in the bulky suit.

"Start the search, Mr. Sulu," Kirk managed to say between panting breaths through the air mask as he passed his helmsman.

Sulu nodded and turned to the colonists who had been watching the events. By the time Kirk reached the shuttle with Lilian and McCoy, the volunteers were spreading out.

Kirk got her inside and McCoy stripped off his helmet and knelt beside her. "I've got to get her back to sickbay," he said as he checked her quickly with his medical scanner. "Only chance I have of clearing her lungs. The siliconic gel is like having glass dust in them."

Kirk nodded. He knew exactly what he was going to have to do. With one last look at Lilian's deathly white face, he dropped into the pilot's chair and prepared the shuttle for liftoff. Thirty seconds later he had the shuttle above the siliconic gel layer.

"Kirk to *Enterprise*."

"Go ahead, Captain," Uhura said.

"I want the transporter to lock on Dr. McCoy and his patient and beam them aboard. Medical emergency. Have a team standing by. Understand?"

"Understood," Uhura said.

Kirk turned around. "Do your best, Bones."

McCoy only nodded as the transporter beam took him and his patient.

Kirk waited a moment, staring at the empty space.

Lilian, the warm, friendly, smart woman he had spent so many wonderful hours with over the past few months. This couldn't happen to her.

He took a deep breath and forced himself to think about the problem at hand. There were others down there that might face the same fate as Lilian. He had to help them. There was nothing more he could do for her.

He turned back to the controls and dropped the shuttle down to the surface. He had no doubt there were others still alive, and this time he wasn't going to be standing around watching a transport take off when they needed his help.

Yanorada was resting in his chair, enjoying the quiet time before the next wave of information poured in. He was also enjoying the feeling of success. Even though he had no concrete evidence that the siliconic gel was forming as expected, every reading during the last Blind indicated it would. And in a few hours he would know for sure.

Relaagith moved up quickly to stand beside

Yanorada. It was clear the younger officer was upset about something, simply by his actions. But Relaagith had gotten upset a great deal over the last few months, and whatever small thing it was this time wasn't going to bother Yanorada. Nothing was going to ruin his good mood.

"Yes," Yanorada finally said, letting his junior officer squirm for an extra moment. "What is it?"

"Six battleships have taken up a position directly beyond us, sir."

Yanorada sat bolt upright and turned. "Our ships?"

"Yes, sir," Relaagith said.

"Show me," Yanorada ordered.

Relaagith moved quickly over to the communications board and brought up the visual images. Then he put a system map under the visuals.

He had been right. The six were Kauld warships, spaced in clearly defensive formation just beyond the asteroid belt. On the map it was obvious they were taking up positions where they could move quickly to defend Yanorada's position from anything that might come at it from Belle Terre.

"Stupid fools!" Yanorada said. Their location was like planting a flag on the asteroid and calling the humans to tell them where it was. Didn't they know that?

More than likely they did, and just didn't care.

Yanorada could feel his anger rising, pushing his good mood away like a wind shoving dust ahead of it.

What kind of stupidity was this?

Who had ordered this?

And were the humans doing something that indicated this kind of protection was necessary? He needed answers and he didn't dare try to get them.

"Tell me they have not tried to contact us," Yanorada asked, staring at the images of the ships as if he could get a message through to the commander inside simply by his glare.

"They have not, sir," Relaagith said.

"Well, at least they are following orders that far," Yanorada said. "But they believe their warships can handle anything. After this is over I will have the head of the person responsible for this act."

"Yes, sir," Relaagith said. "What should we do now?"

"Nothing, of course," Yanorada said, disgusted. "If we contact them we will give away our location even clearer than they are doing. In a few hours we will gather our data again. Let them sit out there. I doubt the humans are going to move against them, considering what is happening on the planet. In a short time it won't matter."

"But why did they do this, sir?" Relaagith asked. "If it endangers us?"

"Because the military mind, and the idiots in charge of those ships believe they can win all battles, no matter how many times the humans prove to them they can't. I'm sure someone back home could not stand the thought of us being here unprotected as victory neared."

"Oh," Relaagith said, shaking his head. "But that makes no sense. We are the reason for the victory."

"To the warlords that believe in might always winning," Yanorada said, staring at the image of the warships, "this action is only logical."

With one more look of disgust, Yanorada turned back

to his command chair. The ego of the military mind sometimes astounded him. The stupidity of it did all the time.

Luckily, in this instance, it was too late for them to mess things up.

Tegan watched as Dr. Akins and two others worked over the body of Len Sterling, a thirty-six-year-old husband and father of three children. Len had been one of the first to come down with the allergic reaction to the olivium. Just a day before Charles had become sick.

The emergency light over his bed had sounded ten minutes ago and they had been working quickly around him ever since. Len's wife, Betty, stood off to one side, holding her hands under her chin, staring.

Tegan had sat with Charles, holding the hand of her sleeping son, also watching.

All the family members of the other patients did the same. All of them knew a moment just like this was coming for them very, very soon.

After a few more minutes, Dr. Akins shook his head and stepped back. All the activity around Len's bed stopped as if a switch had been flipped.

"No, no, no," Betty Sterling said, shaking her head and moving slowly up to the bed as if she couldn't believe what had just happened.

But Tegan knew exactly what had happened. Tegan could see Len's body, ravaged by the olivium allergy. Betty's husband, father of her children, had died from a simple allergy, leaving her light-years from home, all on her own.

And he had died for nothing. Simply leaving the area of the olivium would have cured him.

The shielding in the hospital ship clearly wasn't working. Soon Charles and the others would face the same fate. Each of them would be worked over, then Dr. Akins would step back and shake his head.

Dr. Akins put his arm around Betty. "I'm sorry," he said.

Tegan almost said out loud that she doubted he was sorry. More than likely he was relieved, and would be relieved when all of them were dead. She would even bet that Governor Pardonnet would be relieved as well when that time came. One less problem for them all to deal with.

But Tegan said nothing. Len was not her husband, the father of her child. Instead she held Charles's hand and just watched.

Less than two hours until Gamma Night.

Two hours after that, she and Charles would be leaving the system in the shuttle called *Little Sister.* Since she would be flying blind, she knew no one would be able to follow her, or even know which direction she went in. It didn't matter, as long as the direction was out of the system.

And from the looks of what had just happened to Len Sterling, it wasn't going to be a moment too soon.

Chapter Eleven

"HOW IS SHE?" Governor Pardonnet asked, staring at Lilian Coates on the sickbay bed. Her skin was a pale white and her hair looked grimy and pulled back. The monitors over her head looked level, but Pardonnet didn't know what that meant.

Dr. McCoy stood near her right shoulder and Captain Kirk beside him. Clearly both men were very upset about her condition, but neither was allowing it to show much. Pardonnet knew how they felt. He cared about her as well. Probably not as much as Kirk, but a great deal.

"No change, Governor," McCoy said, glancing up at the monitor, then shaking his head. "She's in a deep coma and at this point I think it's better if we let it take its natural course. There's not much else I can do, I'm afraid."

Captain Kirk only nodded.

"So what happened?" Pardonnet asked. He'd gotten

a quick report from Benny, the transport pilot, about what had happened to him, and how he had gone back to get the wounded. And Pardonnet knew the numbers, that counting Lilian, there were twenty-one survivors and fourteen dead. But no one had yet told him any details about what happened.

Kirk glanced at Pardonnet, then nodded. "As I'm sure Benny told you, we found five of them in the transport."

"Afraid to take off," Pardonnet said, laughing lightly. "Sometimes kids like Benny just don't listen very well to important briefings."

"He listened just good enough to get himself in trouble," McCoy said.

"We got Benny airborne," Kirk said, going on. "And then found ten more survivors in the rafters of the town hall. We had them in the shuttle when an earthquake caused by a nearby lightning strike and explosion, shook us up pretty good."

"It injured four of the colonists, two with broken bones," McCoy said. "At that point we needed to get them out of the area and to a medical facility."

"Benny came back and got the four injured," Kirk said, "while the other colonists volunteered to help us search for more survivors using oxygen masks."

Pardonnet watched as Kirk seemed to almost shudder, then compose himself again.

"Let me tell you, Governor, walking around in that stuff is enough to make you have nightmares for years."

Pardonnet nodded. He had no idea and he hoped he would never find out. "I think the volunteers that stayed to help need bravery citations."

"I couldn't agree more," Kirk said. "Especially Benny. His actions were smart and above the call of duty."

"Understood," Pardonnet said. Benny had been one of his best transport pilots since the first day they had arrived here. He was young and sometimes he was a little too reckless. And often he didn't listen very well, but in situations like the one on the island, he could always be counted on to do the right thing.

"Lilian," Kirk said, looking down at her, "tried to make a run for us, we think from her home, but didn't make it."

"And we didn't see or hear her because of the transport taking off until she was already down and out of air," McCoy said.

Kirk didn't say anything for a moment, but Pardonnet could tell he was really upset. Finally Kirk went on. "We got her to the shuttle, took the shuttle above the siliconic gel, and beamed her and Dr. McCoy here."

"Good thinking," Pardonnet said.

Kirk just frowned.

"So where did you find the others?" Pardonnet asked.

"Spock found two survivors in an air pocket in the old school building, and the other three survivors were the Leigh family, trapped in the rafters of their home. No one else made it. Two died when their roof collapsed on them."

Pardonnet nodded, then said. "I want to thank you for everyone."

Kirk just stared at Lilian.

"Should I send a transport back in for the bodies?" Pardonnet asked, changing the subject a little.

"As soon as the storm passes completely," Kirk said.

"It's the lightning that is causing the explosions and earthquakes."

"Good," Pardonnet said. He hated leaving the dead where they fell. It was always better to give them a decent burial and some closure for the families.

"Captain Kirk to the bridge," a woman's voice said over the comm system, breaking the silence that had again dropped over the sickbay.

Kirk stepped to the wall and, clearly annoyed, punched a button. "What is it?"

"Captain," Spock's voice came back, "there has been some Kauld warship movement."

Pardonnet felt his stomach twist into an even tighter knot. What were the Kauld going to do now? Wasn't the siliconic gel enough?

"On my way," Kirk said. With a quick glance at Lilian, he said to Pardonnet, "I'll keep you informed."

"Thank you, Captain," Pardonnet said as Kirk strode from the room.

Pardonnet turned and stared at Lilian, not knowing exactly what to do next. That wasn't a normal feeling for him. He was usually decisive, but at the moment everything seemed out of his control.

"I'll keep you informed as well, Governor," McCoy said, lightly touching his arm. "I think you've got sixty thousand colonists that need you more at the moment than Lilian does."

Pardonnet nodded. The doctor was right. There were a million things that had to be done in the new canyon city to get people to safety before another disaster hit.

He turned and headed for the door.

"Governor," McCoy said, "make sure her son and cat are taken care of."

"Already done," Pardonnet said. "They are with a good family. Please do send me regular reports on her condition."

"Regular reports," McCoy agreed.

"Thanks."

Pardonnet went out the sickbay door and headed for the transporter room, his mind already working on the next problem that needed to be solved.

"Captain," Spock said as Kirk stepped onto the bridge, "six Kauld warships have taken up a defensive position just outside the system."

"Defensive? On screen," Kirk said, moving around and dropping into his chair. Uhura was at her normal position, Sulu was on the helm, and Spock was at the science station.

The moment the six warships were visible, Kirk knew he hadn't heard Spock wrong. They were clearly in a fairly standard defensive position, wing-shaped, with three on one side and three on the other, spread out over a wide distance just outside the system's Oort belt.

"Any idea as to what they're doing?" Kirk asked. "Anything behind them they are protecting?"

"No, sir," Spock said. "They took up this position and have remained that way now for almost thirty minutes. There is no other Kauld movement in the area."

Kirk sat and stared at the warships on the screen. It was clear they were ready to protect something, but the question was, what? If he could figure that out, he might know the why as well.

"Put a position map of the system on screen," Kirk said, "showing Belle Terre and the Oort cloud, and anything between Belle Terre and those ships."

The map appeared a moment later, showing nothing but a few larger asteroids in the Oort belt.

Kirk glanced around at Spock and smiled. "We were wondering earlier how the Kauld were observing the progress of the siliconic gel?"

"We were, Captain," Spock agreed.

"Mr. Spock, how many asteroids large enough to contain an observation station are between those ships and Belle Terre?"

"Seventeen," Spock said.

Kirk stared at the Kauld warships' position, then smiled. "Using only the two center lead ships as a reference, how many asteroids large enough now?"

"Three, Captain," Spock said, looking up at Kirk from his station. "And two are spinning too fast to be of any use."

Kirk laughed. "I'd put my money on the remaining asteroid as our watcher's station. Can you get it on screen?"

The distant image of a large rock appeared.

"I'm unable to detect any energy signatures, or other signs of life from this distance," Spock said. "But they could be screened. There are, however, some clearly artificial formations on the far side."

"But why would the Kauld point out their observation post like this?" Sulu asked.

"The Kauld are a warlike race, Mr. Sulu," Spock

said. "They would have little faith in the present attack using siliconic gel."

"But since the idea is seemingly working," Kirk said, laughing, "they will suddenly feel the need to protect those involved with it with the military."

"So whoever came up with those nanoassemblers might just be on that rock?" Sulu asked, shaking his head.

"Again," Kirk said, staring at the rock, smiling, "I'd bet on it. And I'll wager the Kauld in that rock are madder than hell at their own military."

Kirk turned to face Spock. "So tell me, how were they getting the information from Belle Terre without our detecting it over the last few months?"

"Any standard form of communication we would have been noticed," Spock said. "So I would logically assume the information was being transmitted during Gamma Night."

"How?" Kirk asked. Gamma Night had frustrated him so much since their arrival here, any thought of being able to communicate during that time seemed alien to him.

"A tight laser beam, precisely aimed the moment before Gamma Night set in, would carry enough stored information," Spock said.

"The Kauld sure like lasers," Sulu said, laughing.

Kirk was thinking the same thing, which was why Spock's suggestion made sense. A short, directional signal moments before Gamma Night would not likely be noticed. And nothing being sent during Gamma Night could be detected owing to the interference.

Which meant that somewhere on Belle Terre there was a secret laser facility aimed at that asteroid.

During the rebuilding after the Burn and the natural disasters, it would have been possible for the Kauld, or some agents of the Kauld, to come in and secretly build such a place. But the question was, where?

Kirk turned to his science officer. "Spock, is there any area of Belle Terre that always, no matter when Gamma Night came, faces that asteroid?"

"I will check," Spock said, and ran his fingers over his console. A moment later the small northern area of Belle Terre appeared on his screen, and he transferred the image to the main viewer. It was mostly ice-covered and barren. "Owing to the angle of Belle Terre's axis, the position of the asteroid is always in line with this area."

"How long until the next Gamma Night?" Kirk asked.

"Forty-six minutes," Spock said.

"So how are we going to find that laser station on the surface?" Kirk asked. "And destroy it in the next forty-six minutes."

"I would suggest, Captain," Spock said, "that we wait until it starts to align itself with the asteroid."

"Good thinking, Mr. Spock," Kirk said, nodding. Any laser station would have to be first loaded with information from around the planet, then aligned with the asteroid. "How long do you suppose we will have to find it and destroy it?"

Spock stood for a moment, then said, "I would say approximately sixteen seconds, Captain."

"Enough time?" Kirk asked.

"Yes, sir," Spock said.

Kirk laughed. "They aren't going to be happy when their information doesn't come through. Mr. Sulu, move us into position directly over the area of Belle Terre Mr. Spock indicated. Then stand ready with phasers."

"Understood, sir," Sulu said.

"Mr. Spock, I'll leave the timing and targeting up to you."

"I'll feed the information directly into the targeting system," Spock said. "Set it to fire automatically."

"Perfect," Kirk said.

"Uhura," Kirk said, thinking ahead to the point after Gamma Night, "connect me with the *Royal York* and *Hunter's Moon*. We've got an attack on an asteroid to plan."

Somewhere on that asteroid which the Kauld military had been so nice to point out to them, Kirk was certain, was the solution to stopping the nanoassemblers. He was going to get it if he had to go through the entire Kauld fleet in the process.

Actually, the way he felt right now, going through them might feel damn good.

Chapter Twelve

TEGAN WELCH turned out to be a much better dinner companion than Captain Bill Skaerbaek would have ever imagined. Just after Len Sterling died, he had stopped by the ward and asked her to join him for dinner. At first she had declined, saying she wouldn't be very good company at the moment.

But he had insisted. He knew it would be hard for her to say no to the captain of the ship she was about to steal a shuttle from. And he had been right. Finally she had smiled and nodded yes to his invitation.

The dinner was his way of trying to tell her he suspected what she was going to try. And maybe convince her, without ever tipping his hand, that she shouldn't try it.

It didn't work out that way exactly. In fact, it didn't work out even close to what he had in mind.

He had decided to have the dinner in his quarters, just the two of them. Since his wife had died, five years before, no woman had set foot in his quarters for anything social. He really wasn't thinking of this as social, either. More along the lines of duty, since there was no way he could let Tegan Welch steal a Starfleet shuttle.

He had become suspicious when she had made a walk-around of the shuttles during her first few hours on board. Then when she had gone back to the hallway near the shuttles four times, he had finally sent Ensign Harrow to see what she really wanted. Again, Tegan's interest had been the shuttles. And considering that her son was so sick, and she felt that getting him away from Belle Terre was his only hope, Skaerbaek didn't really blame her. He might have been thinking of doing the same thing in her position. He just couldn't let her do it from his ship.

When he opened the door to greet her, Tegan Welch looked beautiful, in a very clean, almost plain way. She was only a few years younger than he was, yet looked younger. And more tired. She had her long hair pulled back tight, accenting the perfect features of her face. She had on black dress slacks and a simple white blouse that gave her a very soft look.

"Thank you, Captain," she said as she entered, "for the wonderful invitation."

"My pleasure," he said, indicating she should make herself comfortable on the couch.

"Wow, what smells so good?" Instead of going to the couch, she turned instead toward the small kitchen. A real kitchen was a luxury, of course, but the captaincy had its privileges and he had his hobbies.

He had decided to try cooking lasagna, a dish he hadn't done in years. He figured if it came out bad, the worst it would taste like was plain tomato sauce and noodles.

"Used to be one of my specialties," he said, following her into the kitchen. "Deep-dish lasagna."

"Used to be?" she asked, glancing back at him with a smile. "From the smell of this, I'd say it still is."

"Well, thank you," he said, feeling suddenly very much at ease. He found it interesting how she made him comfortable even when she came to his quarters.

"How about a glass of wine?" he asked, pointing to a bottle on the counter.

"You've thought of everything," she said, again laughing. "I'd love a glass."

"Not everything," he said. "I couldn't come up with a way to make the garlic bread."

"But you have salad, right?" she asked, boldly opening the refrigerator storage area door. "And Italian dressing, I see."

He laughed and from that moment onward, the evening was very, very much off the course he had intended it to take. She helped him with the dinner, helped set the small table, and helped keep the conversation light and full of laughter.

Finally, over the soily dishes and a second glass of wine, she looked at him seriously. "So what happened to your wife? I see her pictures, but no sign of her living here."

"Died five years ago," he said. "Radiation poisoning from an accident. She worked in engineering."

Tegan nodded. "She must have been someone special to be the wife of a Starfleet captain."

"Oh, I wasn't a captain when we were married," he said, laughing. "Just a regular old lieutenant. I had just made captain when she died. What about your husband?"

"Also dead," Tegan said. "A month after Charles was born. A freak transport accident. He was a Starfleet ensign at the time."

"So you signed up for this colony on your own, with just Charles?" he asked. The idea of her doing that for some reason surprised him. She was a very impressive person.

"Sure did," she said. "Wanted a change of pace, a new home, some new memories. I didn't expect to come here, though, and lose my son."

"You haven't lost him yet," Skaerbaek said.

This time she laughed without humor. It wasn't a pretty sound, filled with bitterness and just barely covering her anger. "With Len dying today, it's only a matter of a day or two. The only thing I can do to save Charles is get him away from the subspace influence of the olivium. We both know that. Even Dr. Akins knows that, but isn't doing anything about it."

He leaned forward slightly. "And what would you have him do?"

She also leaned forward, as if she was about to tell him a secret. Even up close, her skin was smooth, her eyes deep and full of intelligence.

"I would have him move this entire ship of yours just outside this system. A quarter of a light-year out for

122

just two days would be enough to give my son and the other patients time to recover."

"Interesting," Skaerbaek said, not backing away.

"Yes, it is," she asked calmly. "There are still four lives involved, and no other patients on this ship. The shielding idea isn't working, clearly, so the solution to save their lives is easy. Move the ship a short distance. That's all."

He stared into her eyes for a moment until finally she sat back.

He did the same. Slowly, thinking.

"What really amazes me," she said, staring at him intently, pushing her arguement, "is that in all my years in space, I've never seen such a callous disregard for human life before. And on a hospital ship besides. It's as if Governor Pardonnet wants my son dead. But that couldn't be possible, now could it? Why would anyone want to kill a seven-year-old boy?"

At that moment he knew she was right. Dr. Akins's most recent report confirmed that. Not about the governor, but she was still clearly, painfully right.

He forced himself to take another slow sip of wine, never letting his gaze leave hers. Then he set the glass down and pushed his chair back. He extended his hand. "Come with me."

She took his hand and stood, her firm, warm skin sending electric tingles through his arm.

"Let's go have a talk with Dr. Akins right now."

"I doubt that's going to do any good," she said, her voice shaking with the anger clearly just under the surface.

This time it was his turn to laugh. "Oh, with me asking the questions, we just might get some different answers."

"Captain," she said, "I'll believe it when I see it."

"One minute until Gamma Night," Sulu said.

Kirk stared at the big screen in front of him. It was showing the land areas of Belle Terre below the *Enterprise* that could possibly hold a laser relay station for a Kauld observation post. It was only the most northern area of the planet's largest continent, and a small chain of frozen islands. The entire land area was covered in snow and in places a thick layer of ice.

They had done a preliminary scan of the area, but found nothing. Spock had suggested that was caused by heavy shielding and asked permission to make sure they penetrated the shielding with the phaser fire.

Kirk had told him to do what he considered best.

So for the last twenty minutes they had just waited.

If those Kauld warships were really guarding an observation post, and if Mr. Spock's theory that the observation post got its information by laser during Gamma Night, then in just a few seconds they were going to melt some ice on the surface when they destroyed that station.

"Thirty seconds to Gamma Night," Sulu said.

Kirk turned to Spock. "Everything ready?"

"Ready, Captain," Spock said. "I'll show whatever activity we have on the screen."

"Mr. Sulu," Kirk asked, "are the phasers armed and ready?"

"At Mr. Spock's command, sir," Sulu said.

The next few seconds ticked by slowly. Kirk watched

the screen, waiting. If they were wrong about any number of assumptions, nothing was going to happen. But as Mr. Spock had said, the percentages were that they were correct.

"Energy spike on the surface," Spock said.

On the screen Kirk could see a bright red spot appear near the edge of a vast ice field. Suddenly bright red lines streaked at it from twenty different directions around the planet. Those lines showed communications coming into the energy location.

They had been right. The Kauld had been gathering data from all over Belle Terre and sending it every Gamma Night.

The familiar sound of the *Enterprise* phasers firing filled the bridge. Twice.

Pause.

Then twice more.

Pause.

Then twice more.

Spock was taking no chances on not destroying the target, which was fine with Kirk.

"Target destroyed," Spock said.

"We're in Gamma Night," Sulu announced.

The screen in front of him went fuzzy.

Kirk hated Gamma Night, but at the moment he bet there was a group of Kauld on an asteroid that were going to hate it even more over the next ten hours.

"Play back what just happened," Kirk said. "I want close-ups if we have them."

"We do," Spock said as the screen showed a barren ice-covered small hill on an otherwise flat ice plain.

"That bump the relay station?" Kirk asked.

"It was," Spock said.

An instant later the camera showed the first two phasers striking the station in slow motion, melting the ice down to the building and then through the thick shielding to the machinery inside.

It hadn't been a very large building, but big enough for a buried and shielded power plant large enough to fire a laser across the system to the asteroid.

The next *Enterprise* phaser strikes caused a massive explosion of equipment. Kirk figured they must have hit the power plant on that shot.

The last two phaser strikes melted the entire mess down into a metal puddle that steamed in the cold air.

"Well done, Mr. Spock," Kirk said, smiling.

"Thank you, sir," Spock said.

"Let's be ready to move at that asteroid the moment Gamma Night lifts," Kirk said. "I want to be sitting on their front step when they wake up."

"Agreed," Spock said. "I'm going to return now to my research on stopping the nanoassemblers."

Kirk nodded as Spock headed for the lift. Ten long hours to wait. What was he going to do?

He sat there for a moment staring at the image of the melted Kauld communications station, then stood.

"I'll be in sickbay if you need me," he said to Uhura.

"Understood, Captain," she said. "I'll have some dinner brought to you."

"Thank you," Kirk said. "Better have enough for Dr. McCoy as well. I doubt he's left sickbay."

* * *

Yanorada stared at his two assistants, then back at his blank screens. "What do you mean the laser *missed us?*" His voice was as controlled as he could make it. "How could a computer-guided laser *miss* us?"

"Something must have gone wrong with the targeting, sir," Relaagith said. "Just a fraction of a degree off and the laser would miss us. It is the only explanation."

"I don't think it's the *only* one," Yanorada shouted. "Maybe it's the one you hope will explain the situation, but it is clearly not the only possible explanation."

Relaagith smartly said nothing.

Yanorada stared at the blank screens, trying to get himself to calm down. This was to be the Blind where the results of his attack on Belle Terre would become clear. If the timing of the creation of the siliconic gel had occurred as he had expected, there would have been at least three major eruptions around the planet that he could have studied for the next ten hours.

He could have also seen images of humans dying under his wonderful invention.

And he needed to know the human reaction to the siliconic gel. Were they making preparations to leave the system? Or did they even understand what was happening yet?

"Sir," Ayaricon said, stepping a half step closer, "I will be able to send a signal to the laser station right before the next Blind, to realign the laser tracking systems. The information missed this time has been stored and can be studied next Blind as well."

Yanorada glared at his second assistant. "Thank you for telling me what I already know," he said, coldly.

"But has it occurred to either of you idiots that maybe the trouble with the laser system was caused by the humans?"

"How would they have discovered it?" Relaagith asked, clearly shocked at the idea.

"Maybe, just maybe," Yanorada said, "they are smarter than you are. Which wouldn't take much, I might add."

Again both his assistants had the brains enough to remain quiet. If they were smart, they wouldn't say another word to him for the next ten hours.

He sat back and stared at the blank screens. Information should have been pouring across them. Instead, ten long hours of nothing faced him like a wall, with no way around, through, or over.

He was not in a good mood. It was going to be a very long Blind.

Chapter Thirteen

TEGAN WAS SHOCKED when Captain Skaerbaek took her by the hand and went in search of Dr. Akins. The dinner had been fun, his company nice. And under other circumstances, she might have been interested in him. But right now her first concern had to be her son.

Suddenly, after she had all but accused the captain of not caring about human life, he had seemingly become concerned. She wasn't sure if she had converted him to her way of thinking, or if he was just out to prove her wrong. But she was willing to go along to see which it was going to be.

They found Dr. Akins in the lounge area, reading, his feet up on a cushion. He was alone and had a snifter half full of a golden drink beside him on a stand. The look of surprise on his face when she came in with the captain was priceless. It was clearly not something he would have ever expected, or even thought about except maybe in a bad nightmare.

Dr. Akins was a short man, with square shoulders and a perpetual frown. Tegan had hated him from the moment he had started treating her son, and she wasn't sure why until after he started telling her the same things that the colony doctors had said. *Be patient.*

Her son didn't have the time for her to be patient.

"Captain," Akins said, quickly standing. "Ms. Welch, what a surprise. May I get you a drink?"

"I think we're fine," Captain Skaerbaek said coldly. "Please, sit."

Dr. Akins did as he was told and Skaerbaek grabbed a chair and slid it up right in front of Akins and sat down as well, leaving Tegan standing a few steps away. Clearly he didn't want her to be part of this conversation, and that was fine by her. She was much more interested in listening anyway.

"I heard that Len Sterling died today," Skaerbaek said.

Akins nodded.

"From what, exactly, Doctor?"

"Heart failure," Akins said, staring at the captain, then glancing up at Tegan. "It's in my report, Captain."

"I know that," Skaerbaek said. "I've read it. But I have what I call an old captain's hunch that the entire story isn't in that report. Am I right?"

Tegan watched as Akins seemed taken back by what the captain had just said.

"I'm not exactly sure what you are saying, Captain," Akins said, clearly not happy with the direction the conversation was heading in. "My reports are always complete. You know that."

"Why are these patients on this ship, Doctor?" the captain asked. "Why was Sterling here?"

"A seeming allergy to olivium ore," Akins said. "The colony doctors believe the shielding of this ship, and its location in orbit, might help their conditions."

"And Sterling died of a complication from that olivium-related allergy?" Skaerbaek asked.

Akins nodded. "Heart failure."

"And the others face the same fate, including the Welch boy? Am I right?"

Akins again nodded without looking up at Tegan. It was one of the reasons she hated the little doctor so much. He couldn't face her, couldn't lie to her face. He knew her son was going to die and kept telling her there was still hope.

"So is the shielding helping their condition?"

Tegan forced herself to remain very still. This was exactly the question she wanted to ask. Having the captain ask it was much, much better.

"It's still too early to tell," Akins said.

The same thing he had told her.

Captain Skaerbaek leaned forward right into Akins's face. "Doctor, when will you know for sure? When they are all dead?"

Tegan wanted to shout for joy and give the captain a massive hug. It was the exact question she would have asked, if anyone would have listened.

Akins's face turned red and he actually sputtered.

The little man swallowed and glanced around, but the captain didn't back away.

"I want an answer, Doctor," Skaerbaek said. "How long were you intending to wait before you were convinced the shielding wasn't helping these patients?"

Akins took a deep breath and stared right back at the captain. Tegan could tell that the doctor was not used to the captain treating him this way.

"This is a medical problem," Akins said. "A brand-new one that has never been dealt with before. There are no guidelines, no prescribed treatments for this. I was using the best judgment I could. I believe that given enough time, the shields of this ship will help the patients."

"All right," the captain said, "that aside, let me ask you this. Are you fairly certain that removing these patients from the proximity of olivium would save them?"

"Yes, I think it would," Akins said. "But we can't be sure of even that."

"So why haven't you asked me to move this ship out of this system to test that theory? Or even suggested that possibility to me? It wasn't until I was talking to Ms. Welch just a short time ago that it dawned on me that you hadn't even planned for such a contingency."

Tegan wanted to rush forward and slap the little doctor, then take his stubby neck in her hands and break it off. He had told her that they would move the ship if needed. Now the captain was saying that he hadn't even been asked for such a thing. No wonder her accusations had struck a nerve with the captain.

"It wasn't necessary yet, sir," Akins said, weakly.

"A man died today, Doctor!" the captain shouted

right in Akins's face. "How much more necessary does it get?"

"Captain, there's something else going on here," Tegan said.

Akins shrunk back, sputtered denials, and then decided to say nothing.

"I'm beginning to think there must be," the captain agreed. On a hunch, he used the intercom to call to the bridge. "Captain here. Requesting a scan of the interior of the ship for the presence of olivium."

"Aye, sir," the reply came back. "Sir," the excited crewmen's voice said on the intercom, "showing significant quantifies of olivium in the cargo hold."

Captain Skaerbaek stood. "So that's it. What was going on, Doctor? Picking up a little spaceborne olivium for your back pocket?" He turned to Tegan. "You were right. Something was going on. This bastard has something rigged to pick up olivium left over in orbit.

"So," the captain continued, "if we moved the ship, and the patients kept dying, we'd know something was wrong. We'd find his secret stash. Is that about right, Doctor?"

Akins had no reply. He simply stared at his feet.

"Doctor, you are under arrest." The captain used the intercom to summon a security team. "You will be rotated to the surface to face colonial justice on a murder charge."

"You can't do that!" Atkins shouted. "I was going to be rich. . . ."

"Yes, I can," Skaerbaek said, staring at the shorter man without the slightest bit of worry. "And I just did."

Akins stared at Skaerbaek for a moment; then the security team arrived and he was taken away.

Silence filled the lounge, and then Captain Skaerbaek turned to her and smiled. "Don't worry. The olivium in the cargo hold will be dumped *now*. Dr. Immi will take over Charles's treatment. As soon as Gamma Night is over, I'll move the ship out of the system. Far enough that the subspace effects of olivium are at a minimum."

All Tegan could do was just stare at him and smile. She wanted to cry, but wasn't going to allow herself to do that. Not until Charles had recovered. Finally she managed to say, "Thank you, Captain."

He smiled at her. "So you won't take my shuttle now?"

He might as well have hooked her up to an electric current and thrown the switch. She actually staggered backward, then looked into his eyes. "You knew?"

"I suspected," he said, trying not to smile.

"How?"

"They don't make you a captain for nothing. I'm sure you want to go check on Charles now. And if you'll excuse me," the captain said grimly, "I have to go talk to Betty Sterling and explain why her husband really died."

Pardonnet walked the edge of the canyon as the sun came up over the desert. The air was surprisingly cold and crisp and smelled fresh. The graveyard shift was just heading for dinner and the morning crews were taking their places. He had three shifts of workers going around the clock, putting the roof over this canyon, carving out rooms in the rock walls, building a sewer and a water supply system. Putting together a town large enough to hold sixty thousand people was no easy task, especially when the time to do it was growing shorter by the hour.

Already almost half of the colony's entire population lived here in one fashion or another. Many were in makeshift shelters on the desert, but some had started to live below. More would move into the canyon today.

The roof now covered a full kilometer of the canyon, stretching off behind him like a flat, gray bubble on the desert floor. It had been tested successfully for leaks of any kind, and his engineers promised him the roof would stay in place in hurricane-level winds.

He forced himself to stop and take a few, long breaths of the morning air, trying to clear his mind. He couldn't remember the last time he'd slept more than an hour, and he had no doubt he wasn't going to get much more than that today. In just under thirty minutes, Gamma Night was going to clear and he would get an updated report of the spread of the siliconic gel over the planet. It was moving far, far faster than anyone had thought it would.

Luckily, the desert area was one of the least contaminated areas, but even this desert would be swallowed by the siliconic gel in three or four days. The canyon city was going to have to be bundled up tight by then.

Also, when the communication lines opened, he hoped to hear if one, maybe two of the mule colony ships were ready for habitation. Both the Starfleet engineering crews and some of his best people had been working around the clock trying to put back together a few of the ships. If one or two of those ships were ready, he was planning on sending a percentage of the people back up there.

For some reason it just felt safer that way. He would feel better if the colony population was in three or four places, but he would settle for two at the moment. And then hope the scientists could figure out a way to stop the siliconic gel, break it down, before the planet became a wasteland.

Two more deep breaths and he headed back along the finished edge of the canyon's roof toward his command center. He needed to be there when Gamma Night cleared.

To his right the sun broke over the horizon, sending reddish streaks of light over the desert around him. Someday soon he hoped to stand on Belle Terre and enjoy a sunrise without having to worry about thousands of people just surviving to the end of the day.

Assuming of course, there was a planet left to stand on when this was all over.

Chapter Fourteen

THIRTY-FIVE MINUTES before Gamma Night was about to lift, Spock walked back onto the *Enterprise* bridge. For the last half-hour Kirk had been in his command chair, going over the plan to capture the Kauld asteroid observation station. Sulu was again at the helm beside Thomsen at navigation, and Uhura was at communications.

Scotty would be beaming back from the mule ship the instant Gamma Night lifted. Scotty didn't know that yet, but with what they were going to do, Kirk wanted Scotty on board just in case he was needed.

He glanced around as Spock went to his station and stood ready. Spock had worked for nine hours straight on trying to discover a way to break down the siliconic gel and stop the nanoassemblers from creating more siliconic gel polymers in the soil. Kirk had spent most of the ten hours in sickbay, sitting with Lilian. Her condition hadn't changed. That might be a good sign or a bad sign. McCoy said he had no way of knowing.

Kirk pushed himself out of his chair and moved up beside his science officer. "Anything to report?"

"I was able to take apart a number of the nanoassemblers," Spock said. "Any builder of self-replicating nanomachines logically puts in a fail-safe stop device. I looked for such a mechanism and found it."

"Great," Kirk said. "So we can stop them?"

"The nanoassemblers can be stopped by an exact, ultrasonic combination of seven sounds. In the last six hours I have tried fourteen thousand, six hundred and ten such combinations without success."

"Oh," Kirk said. "How many more possible combinations are there?"

"Captain," Spock said, "at this rate I estimate we will run through all the possible sound combinations in approximately six years and nineteen days."

Kirk couldn't believe that figure. "Six years?"

"And nineteen days," Spock said, calmly, as if repeating that number were going to make the slightest difference at all.

"Just about six years too late to save this planet," Kirk said, disgusted.

"It was an ingenious fail-safe method," Spock said. "I am impressed by the Kauld construction and creative thought that went into building the nanoassemblers."

"I'm glad," Kirk said, shaking his head and looking at the fuzzy image on the big screen. "You can tell them when you see them. Do you have any other good news to report?"

"No, Captain," Spock said.

"Thank heavens," Kirk said. "I'm not sure if I could take any more."

Sulu laughed.

"Looks to me as if we're going to have to go get the sound combination from the Kauld," Kirk said, returning to his chair. "Mr. Sulu, I want you to have a course laid in that will put us between that asteroid and those Kauld warships before they even know we're coming."

"Understood," Sulu said, "but it will take jumping to warp inside a system."

"Do it," Kirk said. "Mr. Spock, I want you and an armed security team to be ready to beam inside that asteroid the instant we are in range. I want the information to stop those nanoassemblers and I don't care how you get it."

"Understood, Captain," Spock said, heading for the lift. At the door Spock stopped and turned. "Captain, you realize that the Kauld, once they know the station has been captured, will do everything in their power to destroy it."

"I'm counting on that, Mr. Spock," Kirk said.

Spock nodded and left the bridge.

Kirk sat and stared at the fuzzy, Gamma Night--blocked image on the screen. The outcome of what they were about to try might just be the very survival of Belle Terre. They had to find a way to stop those nanoassemblers, and quickly. Even a week from now Belle Terre would be a dead planet.

"Uhura, I want Chief Engineer Scott on board five seconds after Gamma Night drops, and I don't care what he's doing at the time. Don't even warn him. Just lock on to him and beam him over. And I want an open line to the *Royal York* and *Hunter's Moon*."

"Yes, sir," she said.

"Ten minutes until Gamma Night clears," Sulu said.

Kirk went back over the positions of those Kauld warships in his head. The *Enterprise* and the other two Starfleet ships were going to be on the Kauld ships almost instantly, as far as the Kauld were concerned. The *Enterprise* could handle two or three of them, especially with the element of surprise, but not all six. The other privateers were going to have to take a few of the warships on. No matter what happened, he had to protect that asteroid, if the information he expected was on there. And if it was, Mr. Spock would find it.

Yanorada stared at the main screen, still fuzzy. Over the last ten hours he had sat and fumed and planned and then fumed some more. In all his life he had never been so frustrated and angry. His life was information, yet now, at the peak moment of his greatest victory, he was sitting blind and deaf. An intolerable situation. And if he remained on the normal plan, he would be forced to sit inside this rock, remaining dumb and blind, for another twenty hours waiting for the next Blind. Twenty hours without information, and with no guarantee it would come in even then.

That situation was not possible for him to endure.

Since the military had been stupid enough to send ships to protect him, he figured he might as well use them for just that. When the Blind lifted, he and his two assistants would be ready to run full, open-frequency scans of what was happening on Belle Terre. And how the humans were reacting to it.

The scans would give away their position clearly, to anyone looking, but he would have the six warships take up a new position between the asteroid and the planet. If any humans thought to attack the station and stop the scanning, they would first have to deal with the Kauld warships.

"One minute until the passing of the Blind," Relaagith said.

"Ready all scanning equipment," Yanorada ordered. "I want a direct link into the laser relay station first, to download the information there, then a summary of the current planetwide situation."

Yanorada sat back and smiled at the empty screens in front of him. Soon his wait would be over. Soon he would be able to see how his brilliance was working against the humans. And how many of them were dead.

The screen in front of Kirk suddenly cleared, showing the asteroid observation station and the six Kauld warships, still all in the same position as ten hours earlier. It felt wonderful to be able to see again. Someday they were going to figure out a way to get around this Gamma Night problem. The sooner the better, as far as he was concerned.

"Chief Engineer Scott is on board," Uhura said.

"Sulu, put us between those ships and that asteroid."

"You got it, Captain," Sulu said. His hands seemed to fly across the board. The *Enterprise* appeared to jump at the Kauld ships. Kirk knew that Sulu was making a warp jump inside a system. That was not something normally done, but allowed under certain emergency circumstances. And this was clearly one of those circumstances.

"Open a channel to the privateers," Kirk ordered, watching the screen intently for any change in the enemy ships. So far they weren't moving. He doubted if the report that they were moving had even reached a command person yet.

"Channel open," Uhura reported.

"Enterprise to *Royal York* and *Hunter's Moon*. Battle stations. Follow us."

"Right behind you," Captain Kilvennan of the *Hunter's Moon* said. "Already under way."

"Lead the way," Captain Gillespie replied.

"Both ships have matched our speed," Sulu reported. "They must have been ready."

Kirk laughed. "All good minds think alike."

"We'll arrive in position in twelve seconds," Sulu said.

"Battle stations," Kirk said. "Arm phasers and torpedoes and stand by for my orders."

"Armed and ready," Sulu said. "Within transporter range of the asteroid observation station in five seconds."

Kirk jammed his finger on the com button. "Ready, Mr. Spock?"

"Ready, sir," Spock's calm voice came back. "Sensors read three inhabitants of the observation station."

Kirk nodded. That was fewer than he had hoped. Good.

"In range," Sulu said.

"Do it, Spock," Kirk ordered.

"In position," Sulu reported a few moments later. "All stop."

"Hunter's Moon and *Royal York* are taking up positions on either side of us," Uhura said.

Kirk stared at the six Kauld warships spread out in front of him. Behind him, inside the asteroid observation station, he hoped Mr. Spock and the security team were securing the three inhabitants. If the Kauld had not traced the beam-in, then possibly they would not be anxious to destroy the asteroid right away.

"Open a hailing frequency to the Kauld warships," Kirk ordered.

"Open," Uhura said.

"On screen," Kirk said, standing.

The image of a Kauld warlord filled the screen. "What is the meaning of this?"

"I was about to ask you the same thing," Kirk said. "Why have you stationed six warships on the edge of this system? You have no business here."

The Kauld captain looked slightly confused for an instant. He glanced at something offscreen; then his composure returned.

Kirk figured the Kauld captain was wondering if the asteroid observation station was still secret. So he pressed the issue before the Kauld had a chance to answer. "You have no visible reason for being in this system unless it is to attack us again. We have no desire for a fight, but we will not hesitate in defending ourselves. And you know we can do that."

Again the Kauld captain looked slightly confused.

Finally he smiled at Kirk. "We understood you are having some environmental problems on your planet. We were only observing."

"The problems of the Belle Terre colony are not something I ever intend discussing with you," Kirk said. "And our problems are none of your business. Now, leave the area!"

"No," the Kauld captain said.

The Kauld cut the connection. The image of the six warships again filled the screen.

"Target the engine room of that main ship and fire phasers," Kirk said, dropping down into his chair. "Keep us between them and that asteroid no matter what you do."

"Understand, sir," Sulu said as the phaser fire hit the closest Kauld warship.

The *Royal York* and the *Hunter's Moon* opened fire a second behind the *Enterprise,* both at the same time, on the same ship.

It was overkill, plain and simple.

The Kauld warship's screens flashed through the color spectrum and went down. The *Enterprise*'s phasers tore apart the Kauld engine room while the other Starfleet ships cut into the body.

Less than a second after it was hit, the Kauld ship exploded.

"Keep firing!" Kirk ordered as the other Kauld warships instantly broke to join the fight.

Because of the spread-out formation of the six warships, the most logical target for all three Federation ships was the same, closest warship. Again it was overkill as the warship's screens went down almost instantly under the massive assault and the Kauld vessel was cut in half by the concentrated fire.

Suddenly it was four Kauld against three Federation. And the Kauld captain now in charge must have been in a past fight against the *Enterprise*.

"They're pulling back," Sulu said.

"Hold our position," Kirk said, watching as the four warships sped away. "Track them. I want to know where they go."

"The privateers have taken up their original positions beside us," Uhura said.

"Open an audio channel to them," Kirk said.

"Open," Uhura said.

"Well done," Kirk said. "Maintain this position."

"Thanks, but that was too easy," Captain Kilvennan of the *Hunter's Moon* said.

"Oh, they're coming back," Captain Gillespie replied. "You can bet on that."

"I'm sure you're right," Kirk said. "And when they do, we'll be ready for them. Kirk out."

He sat and stared at the screen, forcing himself to wait until Sulu said, "The Kauld warships have stopped outside of communication and scanning range, directly between us and their homeworld. They are holding positions there."

"Waiting for help," Kirk said. "As expected. Put me through to Mr. Spock. Let's hope his part of this operation went as well."

Chapter Fifteen

YANORADA BREATHED a giant sigh of relief as the three screens in front of his chair finally filled with the images of stars again. He stared at the images for a moment, then turned to his first assistant. "Relaagith, are the long-range scanners ready and trained on the planet?"

"They are calibrating, sir," Relaagith said. "Less than one minute."

"Good," Yanorada said. He'd been waiting for almost thirty hours for new information about what was happening on Belle Terre. He could wait another minute.

"Sir," Ayaricon said, "the humans are sending ships this way, I think."

"What do you mean you think?" Yanorada shouted.

"They are moving very fast and are passing our location now, stopping in front of our warships. The big human warship and two others."

"Any indication our location has been discovered?" Yanorada asked.

"No, I do not think so, sir," Ayaricon said.

Yanorada shook his head. "I knew those fools in the ships would cause problems."

"They have caused you more than problems," a human voice said behind Yanorada.

Suddenly human hands yanked him from his chair and smashed him into the ground, knocking the wind from his chest. The pain filled his every sense.

After a few moments, he managed to push the pain back a little and open his eyes. Both Ayaricon and Relaagith were on the floor beside him. Humans had all three of them pressed to the ground with weapons held on the back of their heads. Relaagith was bleeding from his mouth and Ayaricon looked like he was about to break down and cry.

Behind them a pointed-ear near-human watched the screen. Yanorada could see what was happening. The human ships and the Kauld warships were fighting. Suddenly a Kauld ship exploded. Then a moment later another warship did the same.

Then the other four warships fled. Yanorada could not have been more disgusted.

The pointed-eared one moved to the control panel and studied it for a moment, then started working on it as if he'd worked on these computers his entire life.

"What are you doing?" Yanorada demanded.

The human with the gun against the back of his head jammed it into his skin, shoving his cheek into the floor. The pointed-eared one didn't respond.

A moment later another human materialized just a few feet from where Yanorada lay. "What have you found, Spock?"

"The information we seek is in these computers," Spock said. "It will take a number of hours to remove it."

"Get started," the new arrival said.

Suddenly Yanorada felt himself yanked to his feet and turned to face the new arrival. The pain where he had been banged against the floor made sweat break out over his entire body, but he managed to contain it.

"My name is Captain Kirk. Are you in charge of this cozy, little facility?" the human asked, moving up to get in Yanorada's face.

"What do you think, human?" Yanorada said.

"His name is Yanorada," the pointed-eared one said, reading from the screen. "He is the head of the Kauld version of a science department. Also very high in their government."

Yanorada was impressed the pointed-eared one could gather that much information that quickly.

"Well, well," Kirk said, moving up and even closer to Yanorada's face. "Maybe even the inventor of the siliconic gel."

Yanorada kept his face as calm as he could with a disgusting alien so close.

Kirk stayed there for a long number of seconds, then laughed and turned away, moving over to his pointed-eared friend. Kirk put his hand on his friend's shoulder and then said, "Will it be as easy as you thought to pull up the code to shut their nanoassemblers down?"

The pointed-eared one glanced at Kirk, then back at the screen. "That information will be available."

"Great!" Kirk said, turning back and smiling at Yanorada. "It's going to be interesting to see how siliconic gel does on the Kauld homeworld. I wonder if your people will have as much luck stopping it as we are having."

From the floor Relaagith shouted, "You can't do that!"

The human guard holding him down jabbed him with the weapon.

"You are not capable of doing such a thing, of course," Yanorada said. He didn't want to think about siliconic gel smothering his own people. Just humans.

"Actually," Kirk said, "it's already been done. After we discovered what was going on, and that a seven-sound code was needed to shut down the nanoassemblers, it was agreed that you Kauld have just become too much of a problem to us. So using your own weapon on your own homeworld seemed like a perfect solution to rid us of you. Our missile filled with your very own nanoassemblers reached your homeworld during the last Gamma Night."

Yanorada's legs had almost gone out from under him when Kirk mentioned the seven-sound code. It shouldn't even be possible for them to know about it. Yet they did. Clearly. And they had attacked his planet as well.

How could this be happening?

"So," Kirk said, moving up into Yanorada's face again. "We came here to get the seven-sound code to shut down the nanoassemblers you planted on Belle Terre."

"There are a billion souls on my planet," Yanorada said. "You will kill them all."

"You didn't think much about killing sixty thousand of my people," Kirk said, the anger clear in his voice. "Why should I care about yours? This is war and you seem to think that anything is fair in a war, including wiping out an entire colony. So why wouldn't I put your own weapon against your planet? It seemed like the logical thing to do at the time."

Yanorada said nothing. There was nothing he could say. He couldn't believe this was happening to him. To his people.

"I figured you'd like the idea more than that," Kirk said, disgusted. "Take this scum and put him in a room all to himself. Put the others in separate rooms as well. And I want two men watching each of them at all times. Kill them if they try to escape."

"Yes, Captain," the guard holding Yanorada said, yanking him around and down the hallway toward the small living quarters.

Behind him Yanorada could hear his two assistants whimpering as they too were taken.

As Gamma Night lifted, Captain Skaerbaek was sitting in his command chair. He was stunned to see the *Enterprise* and two privateers jump to warp and then quickly drop back out near the Kauld warships.

"Yellow alert! Get ready to move," he ordered. "Plot a course to that location and stand by. I want to be ready if they need help out there."

The *Brother's Keeper* was a medical ship, but it was

also still a Starfleet ship. It had good screens and decent weapons. It could give as good as it took in many cases. Skaerbaek had only once had to use the offensive weapons before, but he wasn't afraid to do it again if he had to.

"Course laid in, Captain," Lieutenant Redmond said. "Standing by."

A few moments later the three Starfleet ships blew one of the Kauld warships out of space. Then a moment later a second. The remaining ones turned and fled like scared children.

Skaerbaek laughed. "Stand down alert and prepare to break orbit. I should have known Kirk wasn't going to need help."

"Course?" Redmond asked. The red-haired young lieutenant glanced around, waiting.

Skaerbaek stared at the screen. "Take us at a ninety-degree angle from Belle Terre in relationship to the *Enterprise*'s position. I don't want to be too close to what Kirk's doing, but at the same time we don't want to be on the other side of the system if something happens."

"Copy that," Redmond said. "Course laid in and standing by."

Skaerbaek turned to his communications officer, Lieutenant Jeffries, a young, bright-eyed woman right out of the Academy before this assignment. "I think with all the fighting going on, I better inform Captain Kirk what we're doing. Put me through to the *Enterprise*."

"Yes, sir," she said. After a moment she nodded. "Sir, Captain Kirk is on the asteroid. He will be available shortly."

"On hold again," Skaerbaek said, shaking his head and laughing. "The oldest problem of a communications society."

"Sir?" Jeffries asked.

"Put him on the main screen when he is available, Lieutenant," Skaerbaek said, chuckling to himself. With all the younger officers around him, he was often laughing at his own jokes.

"Yes, sir," Jeffries said, clearly puzzled.

Skaerbaek sat back in his command chair and thought about his dinner last night with Tegan Welch. It had certainly been enjoyable, right up to the point where she made him realize Dr. Akins wasn't doing his complete duty. Dr. Akins's report had been filed on time, but Skaerbaek was going to wait for a few hours to read it. Let the doctor stew.

Plus, if the patients recovered quickly after being taken out of range of the olivium, it was going to be very difficult for Dr. Akins to explain any of his actions, no matter how well written his report was.

"Captain Skaerbaek?" Captain Kirk said just after his image appeared on the screen. Kirk was standing in a very odd room, clearly Kauld. In the background a bank of computers were glowing, and Spock was working at a panel. So the Kauld had an observation station inside an asteroid. No wonder Kirk attacked the way he did.

"I wanted to inform you, Captain Kirk," Skaerbaek said, "that I'm taking the *Brother's Keeper* out of the system about a quarter of a light-year. We will monitor your situation and be standing by to help at any time, or respond to a medical emergency."

Kirk nodded. "Thank you for the information. I assume this is patient-related. The five who have allergic reactions to olivium."

Skaerbaek was impressed that Kirk knew what was happening on his ship. Of course, Skaerbaek had been impressed with Kirk since they started this mission together. "Actually, Captain," Skaerbaek said, "one died, which is why we're taking this action at this point."

Kirk frowned. "I'm sorry to hear that. Keep me informed and monitor our movements and the Kauld. Any Kauld warship heads your way, you get out of there."

"Won't even hesitate, Captain," Skaerbaek said.

"Good luck. Kirk out."

"All right, helm," Skaerbaek said to Lieutenant Redmond, "let's do it. Only a little slower if you will than the *Enterprise*. I don't want to give the patients whiplash."

Lieutenant Redmond actually laughed. Maybe there was hope for the kid yet. "Engaging one-quarter impulse."

"Perfect," Skaerbaek said. "Just perfect."

Kirk clicked off the communication link with Captain Skaerbaek and turned around. Spock was at one of the Kauld computer stations, his fingers rapidly working over the keys as if they had always used the alien configuration. Kirk was constantly amazed at how Spock could adapt so quickly. Of course, when asked, Spock would say he was slowed down by a certain percentage because of the unfamiliar nature of the computers, but slowed down or not, it always surprised Kirk that Spock could even do as much as quickly as he did.

"Any success?"

"It will take some time," Spock said. Then he looked up at Kirk. "I assume you were playing what you call a *bluff* when you said you had already attacked the Kauld homeworld?"

"Of course," Kirk said. "Good to see you understanding the use of a bluff."

"In this case, I do not, Captain," Spock said.

"Leverage, Spock," Kirk said, patting his first officer on the shoulder. "You bluff sometimes for leverage. Watch."

Kirk turned to the closest security officer. "Bring me the two young Kauld scientists. And don't be gentle about it."

He didn't like being rough on the prisoners, but at the same time, it was going to be the only way to save thousands of lives on Belle Terre.

A moment later the guard shoved the Kauld into the room, making the clearly frightened younger scientist stumble and catch himself on the back of a chair.

"What's your name?" Kirk demanded of the tallest.

"Relaagith," the Kauld said.

"And yours?" Kirk asked, staring at the second.

"Ayaricon," the young one whispered.

"Speak up!" Kirk shouted.

"Ayaricon!"

"Well, Ayaricon, Relaagith," Kirk said, moving up very close and smiling in a very nasty fashion at the tall one, "my first officer over there is having some trouble with my idea of infecting your planet with the nanoassemblers."

Relaagith glanced at Spock, then looked back. Ayaricon just stood, head down, trembling. Kirk could tell the kid was scared. And that was exactly how he needed to be at this point.

"I've made him a deal," Kirk said. "If either of you help him retrieve the seven-sound code for deactivating the nanoassemblers on Belle Terre, I will give you the seven-sound code to stop the ones we used against your homeworld. What do you say, Relaagith? Ayaricon?"

Ayaricon looked over at Relaagith, who was looking shocked.

"Well?" Kirk asked. "You can save all your people."

"I—I am more than willing to help," Relaagith said, "to save my people, but I don't know the seven-sound shutdown code. Only Yanorada knows it."

The younger one was nodding as if a string were yanking his head.

Kirk moved over into the face of the younger one, who tried to back away but was pinned against a chair. "Is he telling the truth?"

"Y-y-yes," Ayaricon managed to get out.

Kirk turned away and looked at Spock, who only raised one eyebrow.

Kirk believed the two younger scientists. They had never faced anything like this before, and clearly had no ability to stand up to the intimidation Kirk had just put them through. Their boss, Yanorada, would be a different matter. He was clearly military and much older. It was no wonder he hadn't trusted his two assistants with the code. Yanorada had known they would give it away at a moment's notice.

Kirk had another idea. Maybe the assistants didn't have the code, but maybe one of them could find it quickly.

Kirk moved over to Relaagith. "I will consider sparing your homeworld if you find the seven-sound code in two hours. Can you do that?"

"I do not think so," Relaagith said, his eyes downcast. "Yanorada's protections are very complete. I would if I could, sir."

The younger Kauld's head was again nodding in agreement.

For some reason Kirk believed that. "Take them to the brig on the *Enterprise*."

A moment later the two young Kauld and the security detail around them vanished.

"Well, Captain," Spock said, turning back to the computer and going to work. "It seems your bluff was, as they say, called."

"Not completely," Kirk said. "We still have one player in the action."

"I doubt if you will get information from Yanorada," Spock said.

"I think I'm going to let him think about his homeworld for a little while, let the pressure build. I'll be on the bridge. Let me know if you have any luck."

"Again, Captain," Spock said, "luck will have no part in this activity."

"Of course," Kirk said. "Of course."

Chapter Sixteen

PARDONNET SAT ALONE in his makeshift office and studied the reports that were pouring in from around the planet.

The siliconic gel was covering massive areas, far more than he could have imagined possible so quickly. One of the settlements along the Big Muddy had gotten overwhelmed quickly during the night and the last of the residents had barely gotten out in time ahead of a wave of the deadly stuff.

Pardonnet studied a large computer map of the world. Red areas showed landmass covered with siliconic gel, pink areas were not covered, but threatened within twelve hours, and there were almost no green areas left.

The area around the canyon city was pink.

There was a little good news on another front. One Conestoga was ready to hold a full load of colonists, and a second ship would be ready in a few hours. Those ships would hold thousands. It would help.

He glanced at the pink area covering the city being built outside his office and then picked up status reports on the construction. All water and circulation systems were in place and working. Construction of living quarters would be finished within twenty-four hours. Enough food supplies were inside to feed the entire population for sixty days.

What the engineers were calling "sonic defenders" were being installed around the city. They were simply massive low-frequency speakers that emitted a noise that broke down siliconic gel molecules. His scientists called it their first line of defense.

The second line was the roof and airlock system, also with sonic defenders installed inside.

The sonic defenders and sealing systems were also being used in two of the major olivium mining operations. A dozen miners at each location had volunteered to remain behind and guard the mines where the olivium had crashed into the planet after the Burn. Pardonnet wasn't sure what they were concerned about, but he hadn't objected. If Belle Terre was to be saved from this attack, those mines, and the mines on the moon and in orbit, would be this planet's future.

He sighed and pushed himself back away from his desk. How had it gotten to this point? He had simply wanted to build a colony away from the Federation, from the constraints of all the rules. Yet his colony planet had almost been destroyed twice, both times saved by the very organization he had wanted to escape.

And now the planet was on the verge of being made lifeless and again he was depending on Starfleet to save the day. The irony of it was almost too much.

But he couldn't depend on Starfleet and Captain Kirk to make the decisions he needed to make now. They were his decisions and the colonists depended on him making them. He just wish he had more choices.

He stood and moved toward the door where his assistants and a group of engineers and scientists were waiting for him. He had no choice. They needed to load the mule ships quickly, and be ready to button up the canyon city in six hours.

It was time to make that stand. Retreating was no longer an option.

There was just nowhere else to go.

Kirk strode onto the bridge of the *Enterprise* and noticed that Chief Engineer Scott was at his station. He was looking tired and not very happy.

"Mr. Scott, sorry to pull you off the Conestoga without warning," Kirk said. "But I wanted you on board in case we needed you in this fight."

"I understand, Captain," Scott said. "But 'twas a start waking up on the transporter pad with Ensign Massie standin' there starin' at me."

Kirk tried to not smile. "Ensign Massie is an attractive young officer, Mr. Scott. I hope you were wearing pajamas."

Behind him Uhura giggled and as Kirk turned to sit

in his chair he noticed that Sulu had his head down and was laughing silently. Clearly they had the same image he did.

He wondered how Ensign Massie was doing.

"Mr. Scott," Kirk said, as he dropped into his command chair, "what's the status of the Conestogas?"

"Two will be ready ta go in a few hours, Capt'n," Scotty said. "The governor has been told."

"Good work," Kirk said. "How soon on others?"

"Haven't even started on 'em, sir," Scott said. "Barely had time to get the two put back together. It will take at least two more days for a third."

"Understood," Kirk said. He stared at the image on the main screen. The Kauld warships were still holding their distance out of communication and scanning range. No doubt they were waiting for reinforcements. And when those got there, they would be back. There was no way they could allow the capture of their observation station to stand. Especially if Yanorada was the brains behind the siliconic gel attack.

"Captain," Uhura said, "three more Kauld warships are approaching the other four."

"That's not enough for them, yet," Kirk said. "But inform the other ships to stand by. We're going to need all the firepower we can get."

It seemed as if Yanorada had stewed enough. It was time to try the bluff on him, before his people's ships returned. And maybe if saving his entire homeworld wasn't enough, the idea of saving his own skin just might be.

On the way out Kirk decided to check in on Lilian

before beaming back to the asteroid. If nothing else, it would make his anger at Yanorada very, very real.

Tegan Welch sat beside her son, Charles, in the emergency ward of *Brother's Keeper*. The seven-year-old was sleeping fitfully, but the new doctor on his case—a young, friendly woman by the name of Immi—thought it would be better to let all of the patients sleep on their own schedule, instead of being drugged as Dr. Akins had been doing. It was clear that Dr. Immi was relieved that she had taken over the case, and that the ship had been moved.

Dr. Immi had also moved all the patients into the emergency area, where their vital signs could be monitored very closely and constantly displayed over the bed. Tegan found comfort in the constant blipping of the heart monitor on the wall, showing Charles's heartbeat as real proof her son was still with her.

Tegan liked Dr. Immi for another reason as well. She didn't promise that Charles would be all right as Dr. Akins had done. She simply said she hoped taking him off the drugs and moving the ship would help. And if it didn't, they would go from there.

Tegan couldn't believe that Captain Skaerbaek had moved the entire hospital ship out of orbit. And that he had suspected her plan to steal a shuttle. The man didn't miss much. She liked that quality in him. And his green eyes.

For the last hour they had been stationary a quarter of a light-year away from the Belle Terre system. The olivium-ore subspace radiation would be almost unmeasurable at this point. If anything was going to stop Charles's deteriorating health, it was this. She just knew it. She wouldn't allow herself to think about the chance this wouldn't work.

Dr. Immi was standing next to one of the other patients, talking softly to a family member, when Captain Skaerbaek came into the room. He smiled warmly at Tegan and moved over to stand beside Charles's bed, staring intently at the health monitor for a few moments.

"Any change?" he asked.

"Dr. Immi said that the heart rates on all the patients had leveled," Tegan said, standing and moving over beside the captain at the foot of Charles's bed. "But that may be just from coming off the drugs Dr. Akins had them all on."

Skaerbaek nodded and said nothing.

"Captain," Tegan said, "I just want—"

"Bill," he said, smiling at her. "Remember?"

She laughed. "All right, Captain. Bill when we're alone."

"Good enough," he said.

She was staring up at him when his eyes got wide. She glanced at Charles, who was looking up at her.

"Mom," he said, his voice soft and rough. "I'm thirsty."

Tegan's legs almost wouldn't hold her. It was the first time in days he had said a word, let alone recognized her. She moved quickly around the bed to his side, grabbing the glass of ice she always kept fresh there and spooning a small chip for him to suck on.

"Dr. Immi!" Captain Skaerbaek called firmly.

Immi glanced up and came running, studying the

blinking monitor board over Charles. Tegan's hand shook as she held the spoon out and Charles took the ice chip and sucked on it.

Tegan watched her son work on that for a moment, then glanced up at the doctor, almost afraid to ask what this meant.

Dr. Immi was smiling. Ear-to-ear smiling.

And so was Captain Skaerbaek.

Tegan had her answer.

And her son back.

Chapter Seventeen

YANORADA HAD BEEN preparing himself for the human named Kirk's return. But when the two guards suddenly pulled him from the room, he was still surprised. He had expected Kirk to let him think about his plight longer. Clearly the human was in some sort of hurry. And that would give Yanorada a slight advantage.

"Well," Kirk said as the guards escorted him into the main area of the station, "I'm prepared to offer you the same deal I offered your assistants."

"And just what might that have been?" Yanorada asked, giving Kirk his best smile. He knew his assistants could have been no help to the humans. Half the time they had been of little help to him and his projects.

Kirk smiled right back. "My people know about the seven-sound code needed to shut off the nanoassemblers you planted on Belle Terre. We just don't have the right combination yet."

"And you won't for some time, considering the number of possibilities," Yanorada said.

The human captain shrugged and laughed lightly. "At the speed of the dozen computers working on the problem, the correct combination will be reached in six and one half hours at the outside."

"Not possible," Yanorada shouted, glaring at the human. The man had to be either lying or misinformed by his people.

Kirk only laughed. "Very possible. I assume we will have the code in the next four or five hours if not sooner. Of course, Mr. Spock over there might find it in your computer system before that time as well."

Yanorada glared at the pointed-eared one, then looked back at Captain Kirk. "You mentioned an offer."

"I did, didn't I," Kirk said, smiling and pacing. "I told your assistants that if they gave me the seven-sound code, I would give them the code to shut off the nanoassemblers we planted on your world."

Yanorada smiled. "Of course, you learned they did not have the sequence. I would never trust such weak fools with such important information."

"So I'll make the same offer to you," Kirk said. "Save us the time now and I'll spare your home planet."

Yanorada stared at the human captain. The man seemed very sure of himself and capable of just about any act. But Yanorada did not believe him capable of wiping out an entire planet full of beings. From what he knew of the humans and their Starfleet, that was not something they would ever do.

"I'm afraid, Captain Kirk," Yanorada said, "that I cannot give you the sequence. You and your supercomputers are going to have to find it without my help."

The human only shrugged. "You are amazingly free with the lives of your entire race," Kirk said.

"Assuming you have done what you have threatened," Yanorada said.

Kirk glared at him. "Many people have thought over the years that I was not capable of an action. They were all surprised. Strap him in that chair."

The security guards yanked Yanorada by the arm and sat him down in his command seat, tying his legs, hands, and chest far, far too tight for comfort.

Kirk moved over and flipped on the screens. "I thought you might like a little entertainment."

The screen showed seven distant Kauld warships. Why was Kirk showing him this? It made no sense.

"I assume," Kirk said, "that more ships will be joining these shortly. And if I were in command of those ships, I wouldn't want this observation station and all the information on it to fall into enemy hands. Would you?"

Yanorada made himself sit very still and only look at the screens, but he saw exactly where Kirk was headed.

"We, of course," Kirk said, "will try to protect this post for a short time. Of course, by then we will have all this information downloaded to our ship's computers, so we will have no need to put up much of a defense. Just enough to make it a good show."

Again Yanorada forced himself not to move, but the

images of the warships seemed to fill every ounce of his brain. Kirk was right. Those ships and the idiots in charge of them would not allow this station to continue to exist, especially if the humans attempted to protect it.

"You should have a front-row seat right here," Kirk said, patting Yanorada's shoulder. "Too bad you won't be around to see the end of your own homeworld. An end you could have stopped simply by giving us a code a few hours ahead of when we will have it anyway."

"You would just kill me immediately if I gave you the code sequence," Yanorada said.

"Actually, I wouldn't," Kirk said, smiling and moving around so Yanorada could see him easier. "I would simply return your assistants to this base, untie you, take the code and retreat. The ships out there would never need to know we were even on this station, let alone talked to you. You return home, shut down the nanoassemblers we planted, save face, become a hero, and stay alive. We get a few hours' jump on saving our planet."

Yanorada looked into Captain Kirk's eyes. The human was deadly serious. For the first time since he saw this human, he actually believed what he was saying. "A fair solution," Yanorada said.

"All I need is the code to shut down the nanoassemblers," Kirk said.

"I'm sorry, Captain," Yanorada said. "My answer is still no. And for the same reason as my assistants."

Kirk looked puzzled.

"You do not have the code, do you?" the pointed-eared one asked.

"That's correct," Yanorada said, smiling at Kirk. "I

would be tempted by your offer, but I'm afraid I can't comply. You see, I had the computer pick the seven-sound sequence randomly."

"I do not understand the logic in doing such a thing," the pointed-eared one said. "A shutdown sequence is built into nanoassemblers in case they need to be shut down. Not knowing what the code was would seem to make such a precaution useless."

Yanorada shrugged. "It would take me a few hours at most to find the computer-picked sequence. I always assumed that would be enough time, considering the function and type of nanoassemblers these are. Not knowing the code also made it safer in cases exactly like this one."

The pointed-eared one nodded. "Logical."

Kirk stared at his officer, then back at Yanorada. The look of complete disgust was clear on his face. He stepped away, walked a few paces to the door into the living quarters, then turned and came back. "Take this prisoner to the brig on the *Enterprise*."

Yanorada waited patiently as the guard untied the too-tight bonds that held him to his chair. It seemed that Kirk was not even serious about leaving him in his chair to watch the destruction. It had all been a bluff. And a good one. It would have worked if he had known the code.

"Three to beam aboard," the guard on his right said.

A moment later Captain Kirk, his pointed-eared friend, and the observation station that had been his home for the past few months vanished.

Pardonnet walked the corridor of the big Conestoga as if he were walking in a bad memory. Or maybe a nightmare. In his worst fears, he hadn't imagined that his colony would have to once again be filling these ships. Yet it was happening.

The halls smelled of stale air and new machine lubrication. The engineers said that all the environment systems were in and running smoothly, the kitchens were rebuilt, and some of the living quarters were put back together. But to Pardonnet, just walking the hallway, it was clear how much had been taken to the surface from these big ships. Large areas of wall paneling had been removed, and in a few places he could tell the decking was temporarily replaced.

Hundreds of people were already aboard and hundreds more were on their way. In six hours this ship alone would have almost three thousand people aboard.

Three thousand people who, like him, never expected to be here again.

He found his way to the bridge of the large ship. There five people were working over panels that looked makeshift at best. And there wasn't a chair on the bridge. Even the captain's command chair had been removed and not yet returned. Pardonnet wondered if anyone even knew where it was.

Captain Branch saw Pardonnet and put down a scanner and moved to greet him. Branch was a short man, with gray hair and a slight pot gut. He'd been a freighter captain for years and had taken this last job with no intention of ever returning to the Federation. As he had said on his application, *Give me a small hunk of land and help me build a house and I'll be happy as a pig in slop.*

Pardonnet had no idea how happy a pig in slop might be, but he had hired Branch on the spot for one of the big ships. And had come to trust him a great deal on the way here. The man was a good captain. And a natural leader.

"Inspection tour, Governor?" Branch asked, smiling and extending his hand.

Pardonnet laughed. "No, just trying to make myself believe this was really happening."

"Boy, I hear you there," Branch said. "I was hoping I'd never hear another person call me 'Captain' again. I liked my little farm on the river."

"Well, with luck, we'll have you back on it fairly soon."

"Real soon, I hope," Branch said, his face serious. "Right now my crops are covered with about fifty feet of that siliconic gel stuff. Not so sure how long they'll make it."

"Neither am I," Pardonnet said. He glanced around. "Any major problems?"

Branch smiled. "Nice choice of phrasing, Governor. Major problems, as in do we stop bringing people aboard? No. Scott and his Starfleet crew did a good job on the big stuff. We're left to deal with all the small things that are important if we ever have to take this ship out of orbit."

"I sure hope that doesn't happen," Pardonnet said, barely restraining a shudder.

"Yeah," Branch said, "but we're going to be ready just in case it does."

"Good thinking," Pardonnet said.

"About ready to button up the canyon city?" Branch asked.

"Next few hours," Pardonnet said.

"Thought of a name for the place yet?"

Pardonnet looked around the now very makeshift bridge and thought about the quickly built city. "Everyone is just referring to it as Canyon City," Pardonnet said. "I've been thinking of calling it Hell."

Branch laughed. "Come on, Governor, from what I hear it's not that bad."

"Well," Pardonnet said, "where would you rather live? Your open, green farm, or in a rock hole in the ground in the middle of a hot desert?"

Branch nodded. "Put it that way, Hell fits."

Kirk watched Yanorada and the three guards beam out, then turned to Spock. "Can you find that sound code?"

"From all indications, Captain," Spock said, "it's in the computer, just as Yanorada said it was. But finding it will be another matter."

"Estimate of how long?"

"Ten minutes," Spock said, "or two hours. I do not know, Captain. And we will not be able to take these records to our computer as you suggested to Yanorada. Such a download would take at least five hours."

Kirk nodded and glanced around at the small main room of the observation post. It wasn't big, but it wasn't that uncomfortable. "Lived-in" described it.

"Are you going to need help?" Kirk asked.

"No," Spock said. "Given enough time, I will find the code. It is clear that Yanorada was not lying when he said he let the computer pick it. Now I must just retrace that step."

Kirk glanced at where the Kauld warships were still on the screen. "Well then, I will make sure you have the time." He flipped open his communication link. "Kirk to *Enterprise*. One to beam aboard.

"Good luck, Spock," Kirk said.

Spock just nodded his head, and as the transporter beam took Kirk, he heard Spock say, "Luck will have nothing to do with it."

With a quick stop to check on Lilian's condition, which hadn't changed, he headed for the bridge.

As the door to the lift slid back, Mr. Sulu turned and said, "Captain, I think you need to take a look at this." He indicated the big screen.

It was instantly clear to Kirk what he meant. Eight more Kauld warships had joined the others. It was looking like a pretty good-sized fleet was gathering for the attack, and they still weren't moving.

That meant they were waiting for more ships.

Chapter Eighteen

TEGAN COULDN'T BELIEVE the improvement in Charles. And the speed of how it had all happened. The other three patients were having the same recovery. They were all weak, tired, but clearly out of danger. Just simply removing them from the area of the olivium ore had been enough.

Tegan just kept smiling at Charles, helping him drink, giving him a little food, tucking the blanket around him as he dozed off again.

Dr. Immi had spent the last hour going from one patient to another, talking with them, checking the readings, clearly not letting anything go wrong.

She moved up beside Tegan and stared at the monitor. "You know, he's going to sleep for a while now. You might want to get some food for yourself so you can be back here when he awakes."

With Dr. Immi's suggestion, Tegan suddenly realized she was hungry. Very hungry.

"A sound idea," Captain Skearbaek said from behind her.

"Ganging up on me again, I see," Tegan said, laughing as she stood.

"Nope," Dr. Immi said, "just taking care of *all* of my patients."

"Thank you, Doctor," Tegan said. "I will take your advice."

"And I know just the place to get a good salad and a bowl of thick stew."

Tagan looked at the captain, half surprised. "You do?"

"Sure," he said, "that's what's on the menu in the crew lunchroom tonight."

"It's the only thing," Dr. Immi said, "if I remember right."

"True," Skaerbaek said, "but it still does sound good to me."

"Actually," Tegan said, "it sounds wonderful to me as well." And it did. Better than a bowl of stew should sound, that was for sure.

"Well," the captain said, "I wouldn't go so far as to say wonderful until you've tasted it."

"I'm so hungry, I don't think I'll notice one way or another."

"Then let's go," he said.

With one quick look at Charles, she walked with the captain out of the emergency area and down the hall. They hadn't gone ten steps when a voice came over a nearby speaker. "Captain Skaerbaek, priority call coming in from Captain Kirk."

Skaerbaek stepped over to a communications panel and punched a button. A screen appeared as he said, "I'll take it here."

Tegan stepped back, but the captain didn't seem concerned that she might overhear.

Captain Kirk's face appeared on the screen. Without greeting, Kirk started in. "I'm giving you a little warning about the situation out here."

"I've been following it," Skaerbaek said. "Looks like it might be working into something major."

"I'm afraid so," Kirk said. "The Kauld have sixteen warships now gathering, and they seem to be waiting for more. And we need to protect the asteroid observation station for as long as it takes for Mr. Spock to get the information we need to shut down the nanoassemblers."

Skaerbaek nodded. "What can I do?"

"I want you standing by when the Kauld move," Kirk said. "I don't want you jumping into the fight unless it looks as if it's going against us. Use your judgment on that, Bill."

"I will," Skaerbaek said. "Thanks for the warning. We'll be there if you need us."

"I know you will. Kirk out."

At that moment Tegan realized she hadn't been breathing through the entire conversation.

The screen went blank and Skaerbaek turned back to Tegan. "Okay, now we can get that food."

"And after that, you're still hungry?" she asked,

shocked that he could even think of food. "Aren't you worried?"

He laughed. "Of course I'm worried. This ship isn't designed to fight, even though we can if we need to. But I've been in Starfleet for a long time now. If I didn't eat every time there was an emergency, I'd have starved to death a long time ago."

She looked at him, shaking her head. "Captain Bill Skaerbaek, you are an amazing person."

"Naw," he said, taking her arm and heading down the hallway, "just a hungry one."

She laughed, and even with the threat of a coming fight with the Kauld, their lunch was good. And she ate a second bowl of the beef-tasting stew right along with the captain.

Trying to be patient was not something Kirk did easily, and he knew it. But he was doing it, sitting in his command chair, staring at the Kauld ships on the screen when Uhura said, "Captain, it's Mr. Spock. He would like you to beam over."

"Tell him I'm on my way," Kirk said, jumping up and heading for the lift at almost a run. "Watch those ships closely, Sulu. I want to be back on board the instant they start moving."

"Understood," Sulu said.

It had been sixty-seven minutes since Spock started his search. Maybe he had found something. With luck he had found the code and they could retreat. Trying to defend a single asteroid against a fleet of attacking ships was going to be next to impossible.

When the transporter released him inside the asteroid, Kirk stepped toward Spock. "Did you find the code?"

Spock shook his head. "I did not. And the process may take even longer than I expected."

Kirk felt his stomach clamp up. "I'm not sure how long we can hold off those Kauld ships in this area. They are gathering forces."

"I understand that, Captain," Spock said, "which is why I'm suggesting I do a mind-meld with Yanorada."

Kirk stared at his science officer, clearly surprised. Over the years Kirk had seen Spock do a number of mind-melds. They were not something Spock did easily. Or lightly.

"Do you think Yanorada knows of a way to get to the seven-sound code quicker?"

"From the way he was unconcerned about finding it, I am certain, Captain," Spock said.

Kirk looked at his friend and science officer. Mind melds were never easy, and sometimes dangerous. The Kauld were an alien race. There was no telling how a Kauld brain would react to such a trespassing.

But there were sixty thousand lives at stake on Belle Terre.

"If you feel it has a decent chance of success," Kirk said.

"I do, Captain," Spock said.

Kirk nodded and opened his communicator. "Kirk to *Enterprise*. Have the prisoner Yanorada transported back here at once under guard."

"Understood," Uhura said.

Spock turned back to the computer and kept working while Kirk paced back and forth across the small room, waiting.

Three minutes later Yanorada, flanked by two security guards, appeared.

"Ah, Captain," Yanorada said. "Time for another question-and-answer session?"

"Put him in that chair and bind him in," Kirk ordered.

When the guards were finished and stepped back, Spock turned and moved to Yanorada, placing his hands on the side of his face and head.

"What are you doing?" Yanorada demanded.

"Just a little question-and-answer," Kirk said. "The Vulcan way."

Yanorada tried to struggle, but the binding held him tight.

Spock's head jerked back a few times as if someone were slapping him, but he stayed with it, his hands in place.

During these mind-melds Kirk always felt out of control, useless. Spock was climbing around in the trash of some alien's brain. Spock was endangering his own life, his own mind.

And there was nothing Kirk could do except stand there and be patient.

He hated being patient.

Finally Spock let go, stepped back, and opened his eyes. For a moment they didn't seem to focus, and then they did.

"Are you all right, Mr. Spock?" Kirk asked, stepping toward his first officer. "How do you feel?"

"I am fine, sir," Spock said, his voice its normal level, controlled pitch.

Yanorada was glaring at Spock as if he were the very devil himself.

"Did you get what you needed?"

"I did," Spock said. "He was not lying when he said he did not know the seven-note code. But I was correct in assuming he knew how to get it easily. It will take me one hour and six minutes to get the seven-note code from the computer."

"You had no right to crawl into my mind!" Yanorada shouted.

"It is not a place I would ever wish to visit again," Spock said, staring at Yanorada until the Kauld looked away.

"Get him back to the brig," Kirk ordered.

After the guards and Yanorada were gone, Kirk turned to Spock. "Was it as bad as it seemed?"

"Captain," Spock said, coldly, "would you like to climb into the head, the thoughts, the desires, of a being who takes pleasure and pride in the mass murder of other beings?"

Kirk could only stare at his friend in shock for a moment before Spock turned without a word and went back to work.

Chapter Nineteen

PARDONNET HAD stepped out of his office to get a breath of fresh air and stretch his legs. At that moment four transports carrying families all landed on the desert at almost exactly the same time. Two hundred people an hour were pouring into the canyon city, with thousands more yet to go.

Plus in orbit the first Conestoga was now full, and the second within hours of being full. The entire population of the Belle Terre colony would soon be in three locations: the two transports in orbit and the canyon city. It had been an impossible task, but somehow they had managed it.

Pardonnet turned and looked out over the desert to the east. In the fading light of early evening he thought he could see the advancing edge of the wave of siliconic gel, but of course he couldn't. It was still a good fifty miles away and his scientists told him it wouldn't arrive at the canyon city until the middle of the night. When the wave rolled in, it would trigger the polymers in the desert soil created by the nanoassemblers, and more siliconic gel would be created from the very soil around them. The first night the siliconic gel would cover the city to a level of fifty feet deep; then, over the next week, the thickness over the city would increase to just over five miles.

There would be no beating the siliconic gel if it got to that stage. Just surviving it. The creation of the siliconic gel was a never-ending process, with all the soil on the planet as fuel, unless those nanoassemblers could be shut down. If the machines creating it could be stopped, then the siliconic gel could be broken down and the planet reclaimed. But as long as the soil was filled with the tiny monsters that created the siliconic gel polymers, and made more of themselves as well, there would be no saving this planet.

He had been so busy that he hadn't been able to think about what would happen if those tiny machines couldn't be shut off. Where would the colony go?

And, more important, how? Feeding sixty thousand people and moving them was no easy task, even when there were years of preparation. Doing it on short rations and without preparation was going to be nearly impossible.

He shook the thought away and, with one more glance over the horizon in the direction of the coming wave of siliconic gel, went back into his office. There was still a lot of work to do to make sure his people were safe for the moment. After that, he would have time to think about the next step.

What would be the next home of this colony, and how would they get there?

If there was going to be another home. They had to survive this, and decide to continue on, before that even became a concern.

Kirk sat beside Lilian Coates's bed in the *Enterprise* sickbay and held her hand. With him there McCoy had taken a break to go change clothes. He would be back in a moment.

Lilian's hand was limp and almost cold. The monitors over her head showed her vital signs low and seemingly stable. But they had been that way for hours and hours now. And that wasn't a good sign.

Kirk stared at her hand and thought about the evenings they had spent together, simply enjoying each other's company reading and talking. Those evenings had been wonderful for him. She and Reynold had given him a taste of something he'd never really had outside his crew and friends: a family life.

They had both known it was going to end, which is why they had both, without talking about it, decided to take the relationship no farther. He was going to leave with his ship and that was inevitable.

She was going to stay and raise her son and help Belle Terre survive. That, too, had seemed inevitable to them. But now Kirk wasn't so sure.

Dr. McCoy wasn't so sure, either. She should have

started to respond by now, come out of the coma, at least start the process of coming back. She hadn't.

And when Kirk had asked McCoy why, the doctor had only said, "She might not be coming back to us, Jim."

But Kirk wasn't ready to face that. Lilian was strong. She was a fighter.

She'd come back.

He heard McCoy come into the other room, so he laid her hand gently back on the bed and smoothed out the sheet. "I'll be back shortly," he said to her.

She did not respond.

The monitors above her head remained steady.

He stood and squared his shoulders. He had a fight to win and a colony to save. He had work to do that she would want him to do without thinking of her. Without a look back, he strode from the room.

Getting the image of her lying there out of his mind took a lot longer.

"Status?" Kirk asked as he strode onto the bridge. Everyone but Spock was in their positions, ready.

"Thirty-six Kauld ships of different sizes and shapes are now in position, sir," Sulu said. "Still no movement."

Kirk glanced around. No one else had anything to say, so he moved down to his chair and punched the communication link on the arm. "Mr. Spock, how are you doing?"

"Twenty-seven minutes remaining, Captain," Spock said.

"Good. Kirk out."

He didn't want to bother Spock any more than he absolutely had to. The minute they had that seven-sound code, they would be retreating to Belle Terre. Defending the planet was going to be a lot easier than protecting one tiny rock in space. If the Kaulds would just give them the twenty-seven minutes, it would be very nice of them.

He doubted they would. It just never worked that way.

"Capt'n," Scott said, "I have an idea ya just might like."

Kirk glanced at his chief engineer. "Go ahead, Scotty."

"Them big, empty Conestogas," Scott said. "They just might be able to help us some."

"Explain," Kirk said.

"Well, we ain't goin' ta be repairin' all of them, that's fer sure. And they all have good engines. Why not turn one into a flyin' bomb?"

Kirk stared at his chief engineer for a moment, trying without success to understand what he was getting at. "Explain."

"We load one with a bunch of the olivium ore from an ore ship in orbit, then rig her to blow at our command."

"And fly her into the middle of the oncoming Kauld fleet," Kirk said, now understanding what Scotty was suggesting.

"Should slow 'em down a mite," Scotty said. "And the olivium would also set off them big mule engines, adding a wee bit to the explosion."

"Level the odds a little," Kirk said, smiling. "I like the sounds of that. How long will it take you to rig it up?"

"The ore and the ships could be here in ten minutes,"

Scotty said. "I'll build a detonator while they're on the way. Two, maybe three minutes after that."

"I'll get them started here," Kirk said. "You get it ready."

Without another word Scotty headed off the bridge.

Kirk turned to Uhura. "Get a loaded ore freighter headed out this way. On the double. I want it here in three minutes."

"Yes, sir," Uhura said, turning to work.

Now the problem was: Who could he get to fly one of the empty mule ships out here? And do it within minutes. Who was in position and knew the ships?

He spent the next fifteen seconds thinking before the answer finally came to him.

Captain Branch stared at the screen with complete shock. Captain Kirk had just contacted him and asked him to do something that was so outlandish, he couldn't even fathom it. "You want me to do what?"

Kirk frowned. "Captain, the survival of Belle Terre may depend on you doing this. I need you to take a few men, beam to one of the empty mule ships, and get it out here to me within the next ten minutes. Do you have a problem with that?"

Kirk's intense eyes bored right into him. Branch had never had any trouble with Kirk in the past, and liked the man overall. But this request was just downright crazy. But with the looks of all those Kauld ships gathering out there to attack, something crazy was needed.

"See you in ten minutes," Branch said, and cut the connection.

He glanced around at the three young people staring at him. They had all heard.

They were all good people, all good at flying ships, all had families and friends and land at stake on the planet below. It looked suddenly if they were going to get into the fight defending it.

Branch knew that none of them had ever been in a fight before, or were even trained in any kind of military service. Their ranks were just for the flight here and nothing more. It was going to be interesting to see how they did if they got into a real combat situation.

In a big, empty mule-driven ship, he doubted if anyone would do very well.

He pointed to a young ensign named Gary Don. "You have the bridge. There are three thousand people on this ship. Don't do anything until I get back. Understand?"

Ensign Don nodded, clearly stunned.

"Bonnie, Haines, come with me at a run."

It took the three of them one full minute to get to the ship's transporter room.

At Branch's insistence they all grabbed flashlights and oxygen masks and shoved aside some surprised family coming on board as they headed for the platform.

Both Ensign Barbara Bonnie and Lieutenant Stephen Haines were flushed and excited by the time the transporter took them to the empty and very dark Conestoga-class ship named the *Northwest Passage*.

"We're going to have to fly her mostly blind from the engine room," Branch said, clicking on his light in the darkness. "Watch your step. They scavenged a lot of the flooring out of here for the floors of some town-hall walls."

"Let's just hope they didn't take the engines and controls as well," Haines said.

"They didn't," Branch said. "I inspected her two days ago. She'll fly. It's just not going to be pretty."

"Captain Kirk didn't say anything about pretty," Bonnie said.

"That he didn't," Branch said. "That he didn't."

Four minutes later the big ship *Northwest Passage* swung out of orbit using only one of its two big mule engines.

By the time they reached the area of the *Enterprise,* eleven minutes had passed from Kirk's call.

And Branch and his young crew had the lights on and both engines working.

Chapter Twenty

"THEY'RE MOVING, CAPTAIN," Sulu said.

Kirk leaned forward and stared at the screen. The Kauld fleet was headed their way. A lot of ships had joined the original four warships. It looked like space was full of them, in all shapes and sizes.

"How long until they are in range?"

"Six minutes," Sulu said.

Kirk shook his head. Spock said it was going to take him another fourteen minutes to get the code. That means he had to stall that fleet, or keep this fight from getting near that asteroid until then.

"Get all available ships on the way here," Kirk said. "Launch shuttles. I want every ship that has a screen and can fire a weapon ready and in position in four minutes."

"All ships are responding, Captain," Uhura said.

"Good," Kirk said. "Put me through to Mr. Scott."

Scott had beamed over to the empty Conestoga ship with a crew to rig up the olivium explosion. Captain Branch had done a great job getting the big ship here on time.

Scotty's voice came back strong. "We got her rigged ta blow, Capt'n. The minute a phaser hits her screens. Or I can blow her at any point."

"Can you get the blast to go directionally forward?" Kirk asked.

"Already set that way, Capt'n," Scott said, sounding almost insulted that Kirk asked. "And the controls are rigged so I can run them from the bridge."

"Then get off there and get up here," Kirk said. "The Kauld are on their way."

"Scott out."

Kirk went back to staring at the oncoming fleet. He had had a number of battles with the Kauld, including before the colony even arrived at Belle Terre. But this Kauld fleet looked to be one of the biggest he had faced. After he had defeated their laser attack, he had assumed the Kauld were finished with the human colony for a while. But the siliconic gel attack and now this proved that wasn't going to be the case. Belle Terre was going to have to be dealing with the Kauld for a long time to come. And the bigger the lesson he could teach them right now, the better off the colonists would be in the future.

Assuming, of course, that Spock found that code to shut off the nanoassemblers. If he didn't, then the Kauld were going to win. And Kirk hated that thought.

"How many of them are there, Mr. Sulu?"

"Sixty-one ships, sir," Sulu said.

"Sixty-one?" Kirk said. The number shocked him. "How did they get that many ships?"

"It seems a few are mercenary, Captain," Sulu said. "And a few pirates as well have joined it."

Kirk sighed. They were after the olivium ore. Join the Kauld, destroy the human defenses, and with the planet already mostly uninhabitable with the siliconic gel, the ore in the moon and scattered around the system would be easy pickings. Made sense.

Pirates and mercenaries were going to be another problem the colony was going to always have to deal with. Whatever ship was going to replace the *Enterprise* next month was going to have its hands full, just as they had had.

And still did.

At least Pardonnet had been smart enough to hire a few mercenaries of his own to protect ore shipments. Those crews were joining in on the human side to protect their best interests. But it still wasn't going to be an even fight. The Kauld had over sixty ships. The best Belle Terre and Starfleet were going to be able to muster was thirty, and a number of them were shuttles, no match for a Kauld warship.

Kirk figured he had a lot riding on the success or failure of the big mule ship, his biggest weapon. It might level the field a little, and maybe even buy them enough time to get Spock off that asteroid with the code to shut down the nanoassemblers.

"Three minutes," Sulu said.

Behind him Kirk heard the lift door open. He

glanced around at Mr. Scott, who moved quickly to his panel, touched a few buttons, and then smiled. "Ready to launch her, sir."

"Do it," he said.

Scott punched the button.

On the screen the big engines of the mule ship fired, launching the massive vessel toward the oncoming fleet.

"Open a secure channel to all our ships," Kirk ordered.

"Open," Uhura said.

"Battle stations, everyone. Spread out in a wing formation behind the *Enterprise*," Kirk said. "We're going to follow the mule ship. Then we'll retreat back to this position and take a stand. We protect that asteroid observation station at all costs until otherwise notified. Good luck, everyone. Kirk out."

Kirk glanced around at his chief engineer. "Mr. Scott, how close can we safely follow that bomb ship? I want that Kauld fleet focused on all of us as a fleet and not avoiding that one ship."

"Match her speed an' I'd say we're far enough back right now, Capt'n."

"Do it, Mr. Sulu."

Kirk watched on the screen as the *Enterprise* fell in at the pace of the mule ship headed out to meet the Kauld fleet.

Behind them a small distance the rest of the human fleet also fell into position.

On the screen it looked like two massive forces were about to collide, and the advantage was clearly favoring the Kauld. Kirk hoped that the military minds in charge of the Kauld fleet would think the humans were trying to use the big ship as a shield. If they fell for that, they were going to be in for a very large surprise, very, very soon now.

"Open a channel to the Kauld fleet," Kirk said.

"Open," Uhura said. "No one is responding, but they can hear you."

"Attention, Kauld! You have again attacked our world, threatened our people. I will give you only one warning. Turn back now, or the ship leading us will blow you from space."

Kirk indicated Uhura should cut the connection and she did.

"I don't think they're going to believe you, Captain," Sulu said, smiling.

"It's my duty to warn them," Kirk said, smiling. "What they do with the information is their problem."

The seconds ticked past slowly as Kirk watched the two fleets get closer and closer. None of the Kauld were turning back. Well, at least he had warned them.

"She'll hurt 'em bad now, Capt'n," Scott said. "Shall I blow her?"

"Hold until my call," Kirk said, putting his hand up.

Scott stood poised, his finger over the detonation button.

On the screen the two fleets got closer and closer.

"They are within firing range of the big ship," Sulu said.

At that moment the lead Kauld ship fired on the mule ship, as if to brush it aside. It was the last thing that ship ever did.

The explosion was massive. Far, far larger than Kirk had expected.

The screen went white; then, seemingly the next second, the subspace concussion hit the *Enterprise* shields, knocking Kirk from his chair with the impact.

Kirk rolled and came up on one knee.

Sparks flew from one panel and smoke billowed from the science station.

The lights flickered and then stayed on.

Emergency sirens were blaring so loud it was hard to even think.

He climbed up quickly, using his chair to pull himself back to his feet. He stared at the screen, trying to make sense of what he was seeing. It was a mess in space, and no one was firing.

Good.

He turned. "Someone get that smoke stopped," he shouted over the noise and alarms. "Open a secure hailing channel to all our ships and shut off that damn alarm!"

Uhura, still on her knees, punched at buttons on her panel.

"Open, sir," she shouted.

Then the alarm quit.

"*Enterprise* to all ships. Return to asteroid observation post area and form defensive parameter. *Enterprise* out. Take us there, Mr. Sulu."

"Aye, Captain," Sulu said.

"Scotty, what happened?"

Scott just shook his head. "That olivium is powerful stuff, sir. Never built a bomb with it before. That combined with the mule engines blowin' was just more than I planned. I'll know better next time."

Kirk laughed and sat back down in his chair. Then he glanced around. His crew looked fine on the bridge. "Damage reports?" he asked.

"A number of injuries, but nothing serious," Uhura reported.

"Mr. Sulu, any of our ships destroyed or out of commission?"

"No, sir," Sulu said. "We were the closest to the explosion and took the brunt of it. All are moving back as ordered."

"Good," Kirk said. "How about the Kauld fleet?"

"They are regrouping as well, sir," Sulu said.

"Put a close-up of their fleet on screen," Kirk ordered.

The image of the main screen changed to show a much closer image of the Kauld fleet. Or better yet, what was left of the Kauld fleet.

The area of space where the Conestoga had exploded was a twisting, spinning mass of blasted and torn-apart Kauld warships. It looked more like a space junkyard than anything else.

"Amazing," Sulu said.

"That packed some power, laddie," Scott said, clearly proud of his handiwork.

Kirk could do nothing but stare for a moment. He had hoped to slow the Kauld fleet down with the mule-ship bomb, but nothing like this.

"How many ships do they have left?" he finally asked.

"I count thirty-seven left," Sulu said. "Many with damage."

Kirk nodded, continuing to stare at the twisting, spinning junk that had a few moments before been Kauld warships intent on destroying them. "Well, that bought us some time and gave them something to think about, don't you think? Nice job, Scotty."

"My pleasure, Capt'n," Scott said, beaming.

Tegan had helped Dr. Immi and the other staff prepare the patients for going into a battle. They had strapped Charles to his bed, even though he claimed he was well enough now not to need it. Tegan didn't agree.

They had secured all movable objects such as medical carts and trays.

Then when the alarm sounded for battle stations, Dr. Immi took up a post at a panel on the far end of the room. Tegan moved to a chair beside Charles and held his hand. She could feel her son shaking, but his eyes were wide with excitement.

"Are we really going to fight the Kauld, Mom?" he asked as the alarm continued.

"I don't know," she said. "I hope not."

"We can beat them," Charles said. "I know we can. I wish I could see what was happening."

"It's better to not fight if you don't have to," Tegan said. "Always remember that."

Suddenly the entire ship shook. It felt to her exactly like an earthquake, only sharper.

Then silence.

Then Charles screamed, loud and clear.

An alarm went off on the monitor over Charles's head as her son jerked upward, then fell back unconscious.

Other alarms were going off over the other three beds.

"What's happening?" she shouted as Dr. Immi came at a run. She stopped and looked at the panel over Charles as other staff came running.

"Damn, damn, damn," she said, working frantically over Charles. She injected him with something, waited a moment, nodded, and then ran to the next bed.

Tegan just sat there, stunned, staring at her son.

What had happened?

She looked up at the screen over Charles's head. His heartbeat was low, his vital signs near critical.

Dr. Immi quickly got the other three patients stabilized, then came back. She studied the monitors for a moment, then looked at Tegan. "From the looks of it, your son and the others were hit with a very high dose of olivium radiation. It must have had something to do with that explosion we felt."

Tegan shook her head. Who was using olivium to fight? It made no sense.

"Will he be all right?" she asked.

"I don't know yet," Dr. Immi said. "That was a pretty intense dose for someone allergic to it. He's young. We'll have to wait and see."

Tegan just nodded. For a short time she had had her son back. Now he was gone again.

Was this ever going to end?

Chapter Twenty-one

KIRK WATCHED as the Kauld fleet regrouped. For the moment they weren't coming on, but he had no doubt they would very shortly.

"Captain," Uhura said, "it's Mr. Spock."

Kirk punched the comm link on the arm of his chair. "Go ahead, Mr. Spock."

"Ready to beam aboard, Captain," Spock said.

"You have the code?"

"I have it, sir."

"Great," Kirk said. "And you are sure it will work?"

"It is the correct code, Captain," Spock said. "It will shut down the nanoassemblers if used properly."

"Good work, Spock," Kirk said. He couldn't believe they actually had a way of stopping the siliconic gel. "I'm sending our prisoners back there, so make sure things can't be used again."

"Already have, sir," Spock said.

He turned to Uhura. "Beam Mr. Spock aboard. And let me know the moment he is here."

"Yes, sir," Uhura said.

"And beam our three prisoners back there. I want them out of my hair."

"Understood," Uhura said.

Kirk stared at the Kauld fleet floating on the screen just outside the massive field of destroyed ships. "Just stay in place for a few more seconds."

"Mr. Spock is aboard," Uhura reported. "Prisoners have been returned to where we found them."

"Mr. Sulu, lay in a course for Belle Terre and stand by."

"Yes, sir," Sulu said.

"Open a secure channel to all our ships," Kirk said to Uhura.

"Open," Uhura said.

"On my mark, all ships return to Belle Terre. We will take up defensive positions just outside the Quake Moon orbit."

Kirk glanced at Mr. Sulu, who was watching. Sulu nodded.

"Now!"

Kirk watched the Kauld fleet intently. Were they going to follow immediately? Or later? He had no doubt they would follow. It was just a matter of when.

"All ships are returning to Belle Terre," Sulu reported.

"No ship reporting any problems," Uhura said.

At that moment the lift door opened and Mr. Spock entered. Kirk turned and smiled at him. "Good job, Mr. Spock."

"Thank you, Captain," Spock said as he moved around to his post. "But I must warn you, Captain, finding the right key to shut down the nanoassemblers was one thing. Actually shutting them down planetwide is going to be another problem of even larger proportions."

"I don't think I wanted to hear that," Kirk said. He pointed at the screen and the Kauld fleet. "One problem at a time."

"The Kauld fleet is moving in closer," Sulu said. "Looks as if they are going to the observation post."

"They are not going to like the fact that their scientist is there, and we were there," Kirk said, laughing. "I wonder how Yanorada explains that."

"I also sabotaged all the equipment as well," Spock said.

"How did you do that?" Kirk asked, smiling at his first officer.

"Actually, very easily, sir," Spock said, seriously. "Right about now the computers and communications systems in the observation post should be melting. The smell should be . . . interesting."

Sulu laughed.

Scotty laughed.

Kirk stared at the Kauld fleet for a moment, then turned to his chief engineer. "Mr. Scott, you think you and Captain Branch can get another one or two of those empty Conestogas flying again? Rig up the controls so they can be flown from here?"

"Sure," Scott said. "Easy as walkin'."

"Then do it and be quick about it. I need at least two, maybe three of them flying as soon as you can."

"More bombs, Capt'n?" Scott asked.

"Not this time," Kirk said. "I'm betting they won't fall for the same trick twice."

Pardonnet stood on the steps leading up into his temporary office and stared out over the darkened desert. He couldn't believe what he had just heard from the *Enterprise*. It was the news he had hoped to hear, but now he was more depressed than he had been.

It was just hours before they needed to button up the canyon city to protect everyone from the siliconic gel. Kirk and the makeshift fleet of ships had defeated the larger Kauld fleet with one shot. And also got the key to shutting off the nanoassemblers.

The Kauld fleet was still threatening, but it was much smaller now.

What had excited Pardonnet even more was the solution to the nanoassemblers causing the siliconic gel. But then Spock said, and Pardonnet's own engineers had agreed, that using the key to shutting off the nanoassemblers was going to be much more difficult than anyone had imagined. A seven-note sequence had to be broadcast at a certain frequency, for a certain period of time, into every square meter of the entire planet's landmass.

Pardonnet had no idea how that was going to be possible.

And that would have no effect at all on the siliconic gel. The siliconic gel was going to have to be broken down by sonic vibrations, again aimed at almost every square meter of the entire planet's surface.

Again almost impossible.

He stared out over the desert around them. Even with the answer to the nanoassemblers, was this planet still doomed? Had the Kauld finally won?

It sure seemed that way to him.

Tegan Welch stared at Dr. Immi. Tegan couldn't believe what she had just heard. The *Brother's Keeper* had returned to a position very near the Quake Moon, the highest concentration of olivium ore in the entire system.

"What is Captain Skaerbaek thinking?" Tegan demanded. "I need to see him. At once."

"He knows," Dr. Immi said, trying to get Tegan to calm down. "Trust me, he knows. But right now he's under orders and in a fight with the Kauld. The entire colony is at stake."

Tegan wanted to shout that she didn't care about the entire colony. That only her son mattered to her. But she didn't. Dr. Immi understood.

And at a certain level, she knew Captain Skaerbaek did as well. But with Charles sick again, she just had to be mad at something.

"You and I need to just stay with Charles," Dr. Immi said, "and keep him stable until this crisis is over and the ship can be moved again."

Tegan shook her head. "I can't believe this is happening."

"Actually," Dr. Immi said, "neither can I."

Chapter Twenty-two

THE KAULD FLEET spent exactly one hour stationed around the observation asteroid before finally moving toward Belle Terre. For Kirk, it had been a very long hour of waiting, preparation, then more waiting.

But as it turned out, it was exactly the right amount of time. Kirk now felt his small fleet was as ready as it could be for a fight. And from the looks of the fleet headed their way, it was going to be the fight of their lives.

This close in to Belle Terre, he had had to assign a couple of ships to guard the inhabited Conestogas. He'd had those big ships moved to the other side of the planet as well, just to get them even farther out of the fight.

During the past hour Scotty and Captain Branch had managed to get three of the empty Conestogas running and the controls rigged through the bridge of the *Enterprise.*

Captain Branch was now standing beside Mr. Scott. Between the two of them, they figured they could fly the three remote-controlled ships enough for this battle. And this time, those ships actually were empty. No bombs, no crew, nothing. Just some olivium ore hastily moved to the big ships in case they were scanned. Ore that wouldn't blow up if hit with a phaser.

Of course, the Kauld didn't know that.

"They're moving, Captain," Sulu said. "Two minutes until they are in range."

"Scotty, Captain Branch, get those big ships out in front of us. I want the Kauld facing them first."

"You got it, Capt'n," Scotty said.

On the screen the three empty husks of ships that had served the colonists so well moved into positions, forming a wedge between the Kauld fleet and Belle Terre and the colony fleet.

The *Yukon,* the *Oregon Trail,* and the *Lewis and Clark.* Three ships that were again doing their duty for the colony.

"That ought ta give 'em pause," Scotty said.

"That's the idea," Kirk said. "Tell the fleet to go to battle stations and stand by."

"One minute away," Sulu said.

"Open a hailing channel to the Kauld fleet."

"Open, sir," Uhura said. "This time they are responding."

"The Kauld fleet is stopping," Sulu said. "Just out of explosion range of the big ships."

"On screen," Kirk said.

He stood as the image of a Kauld warlord he did not recognize filled the screen. The warlord had big shoulders, even for a Kauld. And he was clearly angry.

Beside this new warlord, and a step back, stood Yanorada, looking smoke-covered and not happy.

"Ah, Yanorada," Kirk said, smiling, before the warlord had a chance to speak. "Just wanted to thank you for the information. Your seven-sound deactivation code is working just fine on the nanoassemblers in the soils. We should have them all shut down and the siliconic gel dispersed in a matter of a day. Hope you have as much luck with the ones on your home-world."

The warlord glanced around quickly at the shocked expression on Yanorada's face. Yanorada's mouth moved like he was a fish out of water.

Open, close. Open, close.

Kirk figured that telling them about his bluff would keep a bunch of Kauld searching the home-world for some time to come. Of course, they wouldn't find anything, but it would worry them for a while.

Finally some words came out of Yanorada's mouth. "You're not going to believe this human, are you?" he demanded of the warlord.

"I'll believe who I please," the warlord said. "It is as I suspected."

With a wave of his arm the warlord indicated that Yanorada should be taken away; then he turned back to face Kirk. "I see you have more tricks in store for us with your big ships."

"I did not trick you," Kirk said. "I warned you about my lead ship, just as I am warning you again right now about them. Your people did not listen and paid the price for their stupidity."

Kirk stepped toward the screen to make his point. "Understand that we will defend this planet against your attacks with any means possible."

"And it seems you have enough olivium ore to make your threats good," the warlord said, smiling.

"More than enough," Kirk said. "Now remove your fleet from this system. You have no business here."

"Ah, Captain," the warlord said. "We are back to that old argument. It is you and your people who have no business here."

Kirk snorted. "Don't anger me. We have Yanorada's mess to clean up as it is. I'm in half a mood to send a half-dozen of these big ships at your homeworld and see how you do stopping them. If nothing else, it would be entertaining to watch."

"You wouldn't dare," the warlord shouted, clearly worried about the thought.

"Why wouldn't I?" Kirk asked, smiling at the warlord with his best social smile. "As you said, I have more than enough olivium ore to do the job."

The warlord looked confused for an instant.

Kirk just smiled.

The warlord glanced around, clearly not sure what to do or say next.

So Kirk decided it for the warlord. Kirk stepped even

closer to the screen and dropped the phony smile. "As I said a moment before, remove your fleet from this system. You have no business here."

"And I have your word you will not send those ships against my world?"

"No, you don't," Kirk said. "But the quicker you leave, the happier I will be, and the happier I am the less inclined I will be to do just that."

The warlord nodded. "This is not over."

"Of that," Kirk said, "I have no doubt."

The connection was cut and Kirk returned to his chair.

On the screen the Kauld fleet turned and pretty much as a unit headed out of the system.

Sulu, Scotty, Uhura, Captain Branch, and the others cheered. All Kirk could do was sit there and stare. They had won, and lost only one ship in the fight. He would have never thought that could happen.

"This bluffing technique, Captain," Spock said, stepping down beside Kirk's chair. "You are becoming quite good at it."

"It's all in the setup, Mr. Spock," Kirk said, laughing as on the screen the three big, empty Conestogas held their positions.

"What do you mean?" Spock asked.

"Simple," Kirk said. "Show your power once and your opponent tends to believe you from there on out. That's the secret to a good bluff. That, and a little luck."

"I will remember that," Spock said.

"I'm sure you will," Kirk said, standing. "But right now we have an even bigger crisis to solve. People!"

The celebration on the bridge calmed.

"We have a planet to save. Anyone have any ideas on just how we're going to go about getting a seven-sound code into the nanoassemblers in the soil?"

The bridge was suddenly, intensely silent.

"I was afraid of that," Kirk said.

Chapter Twenty-three

CAPTAIN SKAERBAEK got the all-clear signal from the *Enterprise* just a few moments after the Kauld fleet turned and headed out. Skaerbaek had been impressed with Captain Kirk before, but now he was flat-out in awe. The man had managed to turn back a fleet of ships on a trick and a bluff. Skaerbaek was glad he'd never been in a poker game with Kirk.

"Inform the *Enterprise*," Skaerbaek said. "Tell them I'm taking my patients back out of the system. Then lay in a course to the opposite side of the system away from that olivium explosion area. Half a light-year out should be enough. Engage when ready. I'll be in the emergency ward."

He stood and headed for the lift entrance. By the time he got there the ship was moving.

The conditions in the emergency ward were worse

than he had imagined. From one glance at the monitors over the beds, it was clear that all four patients were in critical condition.

Tegan was sitting beside her son's bed, her head down on the blanket next to him, her hand comforting him by stroking the side of his face slowly. She was one amazing woman. He hadn't realized how much he had been worried for her and Charles over the last hour until just now.

The other three patients all had family either standing near them, or sitting beside them.

Dr. Immi saw him come in. She was talking to Bettie Steven's brother, Dan. Both immediately moved to talk to him.

Before either of them had time to say a word he raised his hands. "Listen up, everyone," he said, his voice carrying over the emergency room.

Tegan's head shot up, her eyes wide. He smiled at her and went on.

"Thanks to Captain Kirk and the *Enterprise,* the Kauld fleet has been turned away. This ship is now moving to a point outside the system that is free of olivium radiation and its subspace affects."

Light applause and sighs of relief filled the room.

"I'm sorry for what this battle has put you and your families through. It was not intentional, but it could not be helped. All of our lives were at stake against the Kauld. And we won."

He turned to Dr. Immi and in a normal conversation voice asked, "How are they?"

"The most serious is Bettie," Dr. Immi said, nodding to her brother, Dan, who was standing beside her. "But all four of them took a very severe shock to their systems. At this point only time will tell how they will recover."

He nodded. He had been afraid of that when the big ship exploded at the start of the Kauld attack. That size of explosion could only have been done with olivium.

He moved from bed to bed, patient to patient, family to family, intentionally leaving Tegan and Charles to last.

When he got there she reached up and he took her hand.

She squeezed his hand and he sat down beside her, holding her soft hand in his.

"Thank you," she said.

"For what?" Her thanks surprised him. He had been afraid she would be angry at him.

"I know you kept all our best interests in mind the entire time. I know there was nothing you could do, except what you are doing now. It's more than I could have hoped for a day ago. So thank you."

He squeezed her hand and together they sat with Charles, watching the monitor and waiting. There was nothing else either of them could now do.

Benny felt pride in the fact that he was going to be the first to kill nanoassemblers. What an honor. He took the transport in at the exact height needed over the test area, making sure the coded sound was on and everything was working as it should be.

All instruments registered on the money.

Perfect.

Near the edge of the canyon city, Governor Pardonnet, Captain Kirk, the Vulcan Spock, and a dozen others stood, watching him make this pass. It was the first test of the system to stop the nanoassemblers. And the governor had picked him to do it.

He ran the short test area, swung the transport around as he had been instructed, and then ran a second strip beside the first. At the moment he was only covering a thirty-paces-wide area. Not much, but enough for the test, they told him.

After his second pass he brought the transport in for a landing with a flourish, making sure all the new equipment was shut down as he'd been told it should be.

Captain Kirk and the governor strode toward him, greeting him as he got out. "Nicely done, Benny," Kirk said.

"Thank you, Captain."

Benny beamed as together the three of them headed for where Spock and the other colony scientists were digging in the test area, then studying what they found with special scanners designed only to spot live nanoassemblers.

"Well?" Kirk asked, moving up beside the Vulcan.

"It seems, Captain," Spock said, "that the test has been successful."

"All right!" Benny said, pumping his fist. Then he looked at the governor. "What's next? It's going to be pretty much impossible to cover the entire planet like I just did."

"But for the moment," Kirk said, "that's exactly what we're going to have to do. We're going to put this device and a sonic disruptor to destroy the siliconic gel on every transport and every shuttle that can fly low. For now it's going to be a defensive war. We've got to clear the siliconic gel from the colony areas, farmlands, and forests as soon as possible."

Spock nodded. "It should be possible in thirty hours to construct a larger device that will be mounted on the *Enterprise* and other ships and cover a two-hundred-mile-wide strip."

Kirk patted Benny on the back. "But until then, it's going to be up to you and everyone who can fly a transport to start clearing important areas."

Benny smiled at the captain. "Just tell me where to fly and how low."

Kirk laughed. "I knew I liked you for a reason."

Kirk walked into the *Enterprise* sickbay and knew at once that something wasn't right.

Lilian was still on the bed, the monitor over her head looked normal, but McCoy was now sitting at the foot of her bed, just staring at her.

McCoy looked up as he entered, then looked back at Lilian. "You know," McCoy said, "I always really liked her."

"I know," Kirk said. And he had always known. At first he felt odd that Lilian had wanted to spend time with him, instead of McCoy. But McCoy hadn't even tried to spend time with her, so it had just happened. Yet it had always been clear what the doctor's feelings were about her, right from the start.

Kirk moved over and stood next to Lilian. "What's happened?"

"She's not going to make it," McCoy said, his voice soft.

Kirk felt as if someone had kicked him in the stomach. He stepped back and sat down in a nearby chair, staring first at her, then at McCoy. He knew better than to ask the doctor if he was certain. When it came to Lilian, McCoy would always be certain. He hadn't moved from her side for the entire time she was here.

"How long?" Kirk finally managed to ask. His voice sounded hollow to his own ears. He didn't want to know the answer, but he had to.

McCoy sighed and stood. Slowly he moved around to the side of the bed, as if walking in thick mud. Then, without looking at Kirk, he clicked off a switch.

All of Lilian's vital signs flatlined on the monitor over the bed.

"I was just keeping her heart and lungs working the past hour on the machine. She's been brain-dead for a few hours now."

The two men stared over Lilian's lifeless body, neither looking at the other, neither wanting to let her go just yet.

Kirk sat there and thought back over the time he had spent with her, the nights reading and talking in her cabin, the hours worrying about her, the bravery it took when she saved the children during the Burn.

Poor Reynold. Kirk would have to break the news to the boy. Lilian would want that.

Lilian. How was it possible she wasn't with them anymore?

He stared at her body and right at that moment, more

than anything else, he wanted to be away from this colony, this planet, and all its problems.

He wanted to go to the bridge and turn the *Enterprise* toward home and just forget.

Forget Lilian.

Forget Belle Terre.

Forget it all.

And the day he could do that would not come soon enough now for him.

He stood and moved around her body to McCoy. He put a hand on his friend's shoulder. "You did everything you could."

"I know," McCoy said. "And I'm sorry that wasn't enough."

Chapter Twenty-four

KIRK SAT in his command chair and studied the image of Belle Terre on the screen in front of him. "Are all ships in position, Mr. Sulu?" Kirk asked.

"They are, sir," Sulu said.

"Mr. Spock, are you ready?"

"Yes," Spock said.

Kirk stared at the beautiful blues and whites and greens of Belle Terre below him. In the last twenty hours Spock had managed to figure out a way to rig up a sonic emitter that would break down the siliconic gel and deactivate the nanoassemblers at the same time.

Two birds in one swipe, so to speak.

The equipment was now installed in ten ships, which would spend the next three days covering every inch of the Belle Terre surface at least ten times. Spock had said that five times would be enough, but then agreed that if even one nanoassembler was missed, the entire problem could return.

So they were going to cover the planet ten different times, from ten different angles, on a pattern that would allow as many ships as possible to cover each mile of ground.

In three days there wouldn't be a nanoassembler or a molecule of siliconic gel left on the planet. And not soon enough as far as Kirk was concerned.

He bet it wouldn't be soon enough for all the people still living in the big mule ships, waiting to return to their homes. They would be the happy ones when this was over.

"Ready when you are, Mr. Spock," Kirk said.

"All ships report ready, sir," Spock said.

"Then let's get this started. On my mark. Now!"

Below them the seven-sound code shut down nanoassemblers by the billions and smashed the siliconic gel molecules back into their natural components.

Kirk watched as the planet's surface slowly moved past under the *Enterprise*. It was going to be a long three days, but to save this colony, a worthwhile three days.

The medical emergency room of the *Brother's Keeper* was both a happy place and a somber one. All the patients but Charles had recovered from the shock of the olivium explosion. For some reason that Dr. Immi couldn't explain, Charles wasn't responding as well.

So for the last two days Tegan had been at her son's side, with Dr. Immi and Captain Skaerbaek never far away. This morning she was half dozing, her head on the edge of the bed beside Charles, when as if in a dream she heard him say, "Mom, did we win? Did we beat the Kauld fleet?"

Captain Skaerbaek, who had spent most of the last two days sitting with her beside Charles, laughed, jumped to his feet, and shouted for Dr. Immi.

Tegan came right up out of her chair, hoping against hope that what she had heard hadn't been a dream.

It hadn't been.

Charles was lying there, looking at her, expecting her to answer his question about the fight with the Kauld. It was clearly the last thing he remembered.

Without realizing what she was doing, she was over Charles, hugging him and kissing his cheek. For the second time, her son had been given back to her. She was going to do everything in her power to make sure he wasn't taken a third time. And she knew Captain Skaerbaek would also.

Dr. Immi managed to push her aside long enough to do a quick check of Charles; then the doctor smiled. "I think he's going to be all right."

"I'm just tired is all," Charles said. "Did we win? I must have fallen asleep."

Tegan reached over and hugged the firm, hard shoulders of Captain Skaerbaek, then smiled at her son. "We won."

"I knew you could do it, Captain," Charles said, smiling at Captain Skaerbaek

"So did I," Tegan said, looking up at the captain's beaming face. "So did I."

* * *

Kirk walked down the sand dune to the spot where he remembered watching Lilian supervise children, seemingly a lifetime before. The sea was rough, the air full of salt and brine. But at least it wasn't covered with siliconic gel. That was gone.

The nanoassemblers were gone.

The planet was recovering nicely, just as it had done after the Burn.

A lot of things had changed since that day he watched her here. A lot of things were the same.

The colonists were back in their homes, their crops, for the most part, growing again. Life was moving on almost as if this last attack hadn't happened. Everything almost seemed the same.

Except for Lilian.

He stared down at the empty beach. She was gone and he just couldn't quite get a handle on that fact for some reason. Over the years he'd lost many friends and fellow crew. Some he accepted, others he never did.

Lilian's death was going to be one he'd never accept. To him she had always been too alive, too vibrant, too much a part of the colony life ever to die.

He had saved the colony three times now. But he couldn't save Lilian.

He took a deep breath of the salt-filled air and wondered what would eventually become of this colony. Soon he would be taking the *Enterprise* back to Federation space. That was a long distance off and it was going to be hard to keep up with the events going on here. He knew he would try.

And he would follow how Reynold was doing as

best he could. She had raised a good son. The boy had been devastated by the news, but he had known the risks. He had said so, tearfully, trying to be strong. Governor Pardonnet had already chosen a family to take care of the boy. They were good people, but they weren't Lilian. Still, she had given Reynold a strong foundation. In time, the kid would be all right.

Kirk stared out over the ocean. He was going to miss this planet at times. But with Lilian gone, he wasn't going to miss it as much as he would have.

He turned his back on the ocean and moved back up the dune toward the colony beyond. There was still a lot of work to do before he could head home. This afternoon he had meetings with the governor and his scientists. After that he needed to help set up a shipping system to get the olivium ore back to the Federation safely.

Lots and lots of work to do.

Of course, with a colony, there was always a lot of work to do. It just seemed that with Belle Terre, there was always more than normal.

**Pocket Books
Proudly Presents**

**STAR TREK®
NEW EARTH #6
*CHALLENGER***

Diane Carey

Available from Pocket Books

**Turn the page for a preview of
*Challenger. . . .***

Turn the page for a preview of
Challenger...

"How could threat vessels get so close without tripping our sensors?"

"What do you expect from me? Look at the monitors. Completely gamma-seized."

"Then we better saddle up and learn to ride blind."

The sci-deck of Starfleet Cruiser *Peleliu* stank and smoldered. Part of the carpet was on fire, but nobody was bothering with it. Hot damage crawled like parasites through the mechanics under the sensor boards' tripolymer skin. Burst connections caused tiny volcanoes of acid in ripped-open sheeting. A third of the pressure pads and readouts had quit working or were crying for damage control.

Nick Keller swiped his uniform's dirty sleeve across his forehead, bent over the sensor boards, and tried to focus his stinging eyes. A fleck of insulation hung from a wing of his briar-patch-brown hair and blocked part of his view. For an hour they'd fielded attacks from enemies they couldn't see, couldn't target, and hadn't expected. How had any hostiles known they were on their way out to Belle Terre? Or was this some new enemy that nobody in Starfleet or out at the colony even knew about yet?

The question went unanswered. Sensors couldn't see through the bath of gamma radiation spewed by a pulsing neutron star so far away that even working long-range sensors wouldn't have picked it up.

Beside him, Tim McAddis dribbled sweat from his pale forehead onto the sensor dials. His blond hair glistened with a frost of perspiration. "I'm used to seeing things a solar system away, not a lousy five hundred yards. Now that our deflectors are on full, we can't even pick up phantom data like before."

It was a hard thing for a science officer to admit.

Keller pressed a hand to McAddis's hunched shoulder. "Look at the bright side. You'll get the blame instead of me."

McAddis grinned nervously. "The mighty second mate stands defiant."

A knock on the cold-molded lattice grid near his knee got Keller's attention. He found the first officer's reassuring face peering up from the command deck seven feet below, through the lattice fence that prevented crewmen or tools from falling under the sci-deck rail. "What've you two got up there? How'd they come up on us?"

Without a good explanation, Keller knelt to meet him under the rail and handed over the unhelpful truth. "Derek, they must've cruised in cold. No engines. Coasting, like the old days of rocketry. We were looking for exhaust signatures, not solid objects. All I can figure is the bad guys are accustomed to blackout action and know how to maneuver on inertia. Without engines, they're really invisible."

"Mr. Hahn," the communications officer interrupted, "sickbay reports thirty casualties."

"How many dead?" Derek Hahn asked.

"They just said casualties. I don't think they want to tell us."

Kneeling up here in only a pretense of seclusion, Keller gripped the rail at the tremor in Tracy Chan's voice. Everybody was shaken badly. They weren't even sure yet how many of their shipmates were dead. Suj Sanjai at tactical had been killed in the first hit less than an hour ago. That grim hello had brought in critical seconds of attack before the *Peleliu* got its shields up. Since then, the minutes had been long and bitter, landing percussion after percussion on them from unseen foes who understood better than Starfleet how to fight during Gamma Night.

"Phasers direct aft," the captain ordered. "Fire!"

Both Keller and Hahn looked at the command deck.

Staccato phaser fire spewed from the aft array, at targets no one could see, jolting the ship much more than normal. That was the damage speaking. The cruiser convulsed under Keller's knee.

Keeping his voice low, he murmured, "What's he targeting? He can't possibly know where they are."

Hahn shook his head, but said nothing. He watched Captain Roger Lake, stalking the center deck.

From up here on the half-circle balcony, Keller clearly saw the command arena below except for the turbolift. The science and engineering balcony where he knelt rested on top of the lift's tube structure, a design meant to maximize use of the cruiser's support skeleton. Two narrow sets of ladder steps, one to his left and the other to his right, curved down to the command deck on either side of the lift doors. Below, Crewman Makarios at the helm and Ensign Hurley at nav both hunched over their controls, staring at the main viewscreen, which stubbornly showed them only a static field interrupted every twenty seconds or so by a grainy flash of open space, fed by McAddis's tedious attempts to clear the sensors. The largest screen on the bridge—on any Starfleet bridge—was their window to eternity. The two fellows at the helm were hoping for a lucky glimpse of the attackers, maybe get off a clean shot with full phasers.

To port of the helm the half-demolished tactical station was still unmanned, with Captain Lake's stocky form haunting it as he tried to keep one eye on the main screen. Why hadn't he called for somebody to replace Sanjai? Why was he so moody?

To starboard, Chan's communications console was the only board on the bridge that had so far evaded damage, either direct or repercussive. Everybody else was struggling just to make things work at half capacity. Those first hits had done some nasty work.

Up here the engineering console on the balcony's starboard side beeped madly, reporting dozens of damaged sites all over the ship, but there was no one to answer. The engineers had split for their own section as soon as the attack came, and behind him the environmental and life-support board went wanting too. Keller and McAddis were up here alone.

Almost alone.

The sci-deck offered a certain amount of privacy. Sound insulation and clever design of the ceiling shell prevented travel of much conversation from up here to the lower deck, where command conversations were also taking place. The two sections, then, could be functionally close, but not interrupt each other. Usually, Keller liked it up here. This was second-officer territory if ever there had been any. During this voyage, though, an added presence haunted the upper deck.

He glanced to his right.

There she was. That Rassua woman, Zoa, along for the haul. A cross between an ambassador and an inspector, she wasn't in Starfleet, but she was here most of the time anyway, fulfilling her mission of "determining whether the Federation is up the standards of the Rassua."

She stood on the upper deck as if someone had leaned an ancient Egyptian sarcophagus against the console, both legs braced, her gold face and thick hair in a waterfall of severe skinny plaits, her lined lips giving nothing away. In the months of travel, Keller had only heard her voice a couple of times. If she was any indication, the Rassua weren't talkative.

Dressed in woven strips of leather that left her heavily tattooed shoulders bare, Zoa was markedly disparate from the Starfleet crew in their black trousers and brick-red jackets. If only she had boots on. Instead, she wore only some kind of crisscross thong sandals with thick soles, allowing her two-inch toenails to curve down like a hawk's talons hooked over a branch.

And she never moved her face. Her blue-dot eyes followed the crew action here and below. It was like having a sphinx watch every move they made. Keller wished he could order her off the bridge. Roger Lake wanted her here. He liked showing off to an alien who was being courted by the Federation. The UFP wanted the Rassua alliance to guard their zenith borders.

So here she was, observing. If they got out of this, she'd have a real story for somebody back home.

Keller had hoped she'd get the hint and go below when the battle started, but apparently this was what she'd been waiting for all along and she wasn't about to leave. He tried to ignore her. His skull throbbed.

Derek Hahn reached up and caught Keller's wrist. "You okay? Your left eye's dilating."

His swollen temple ached under Keller's probing fingers. "Feel like I got mule-kicked."

"You got ship-kicked. For a minute there I didn't think

we'd come out of that spin. Harrison's hands are full in sickbay, but I'll have Ring come up here."

"No, don't. Savannah's a passenger this trip. She shouldn't have to be on the bridge."

"Won't hurt a Starfleet medic to work her passage. She wants to start a Special Services Rescue Unit at Belle Terre, she can start right here."

"Were you a drill sergeant in a previous life?"

"Everybody needs a hobby." Hahn looked under the sci-deck balcony toward the communications post. "Tracy, call Savannah Ring to the bridge with her bag of tricks."

"Aye, sir. Medic Ring, report to the bridge with a field kit. Medic Ring to the bridge, please."

"Nick!" McAddis erupted from the science board. "I'm getting a shadow! I think they're coming in again!"

Without even attempting to confirm the readings, Keller glanced at the stocky form of their captain, pacing the lower deck between the helm and the command chair. "Tell him, Derek."

Accepting Keller's instincts, Hahn spun around. "Captain, brace for another pass!"

On the command deck, Captain Roger Lake didn't order the crew to brace or any other preventive action. Instead he made a completely unexplained order. "Thrusters on! One-eighth impulse power!"

Hahn stepped away from the rail and croaked, "Sir, we shouldn't be moving during Gamma Night!"

Lake shot him a glare. "We've got to outrun them while we can. I know how these people think."

Keller pushed to his feet and spoke up, "Sir, I agree with Derek. One full-power hit from *Peleliu* would demolish any ship in this sector. They don't have anything that can match—"

"They've got everything we've got. Fire!"

Lake's eyes were fixed on the forward screen, as if he saw something there. But there was nothing. Only a clicking blue cloud of static. Yet he was shooting, over and over, depleting their weapons, sending unthinkable destructive power racing through space behind them without effect.

Hahn came back to the rail and peered up at McAddis's scanners. "If only we could go to warp speed . . ."

Gamma Night laughed in his face.

Hahn turned to watch Lake from behind, analyzing the set of the captain's shoulders, the quick breathing, the cranky movements, the petulant glances. "We're dead if we keep moving." He jumped to the nearest ladder, climbed it, and joined Keller at the suffering sensors. His voice was very low. "He's snapping, Nick."

Cold dread washed down Keller's spine. He glanced to his side, afraid the science officer had overheard, but McAddis had moved down the sensor bank and was preoccupied.

Keller's hands turned icy. "Now, let's not pick our peaches before they're fuzzy."

"We gambled," Hahn said. "We lost."

"We don't know that yet, Dee," Keller downplayed.

"His judgments are sluggish, he's irrational—this stuff about how they've got everything we've got—who does he think is out there?"

Desperate to hold together whatever they had, Keller resisted the urge to face him and obviously be having a conversation that might get the captain's attention. Quietly he said, "Harrison did a psych scan two weeks ago for chemical abnormalities. The results were indeterminate. This is just stress. He hasn't been in battle for years."

"Neither have I, but I'm not—"

"Hey, I've got blips on the short-range," McAddis interrupted. "I think they might be moving away!"

Keller spoke past Hahn. "Captain, they might be moving off."

"If we hold off on weapons fire," Hahn added, "they might lose us. Sir!"

"Don't believe the equipment!" Lake whirled around, meeting everyone's eyes one by one. "They've done something to our sensors! Sabotage. We have to rely on instinct. We know they always attack in a wedge formation. Like bees."

At that, Hahn stepped forward. "Captain, how can you recognize something we've never encountered before?"

"Don't joke around, Dee," Lake said. "It's typical Klingon formation. Hurley, did I tell you to stop shooting?"

Beside Keller, McAddis bent forward as if he'd gotten a cramp. *"Klingons."*

"Shh. Anybody can misspeak. He means Kauld."

But he peered past Hahn, down to the command area. A

few steps to their right, the Rassua woman now had her inkdot eyes fixed not on Lake, but on Keller and Hahn. Gold face, a zillion little braids, and eyes with no pupils, just solid blue, grilling them with an angry message.

This could get out of hand. Turning away from her, Keller pressed a couple of fingers gingerly to his aching head and used the other hand to play the suffering sensors, but he overturned the dial and lost the image.

McAddis nudged him. "All right, Nick?"

Beside them, Hahn complained, "What's taking Ring so long?"

Keller waved them off. "Swamped in sickbay. I'll just put a patch over the dilated one. You can call me the Santa Fe Bandito."

McAddis smiled, then murmured, "I'd feel better if *she* just wasn't here all the time."

"Captain likes having her here, watching," Hahn reminded, almost casting a glance back at Zoa, then changing his mind at the last second. "Her people have a taste for frontier living. They weren't interested in the UFP before Belle Terre broke wide open."

"Funny," Keller commented. "Nobody wanted to go out there when it was peaceful and pretty. Now hell's broke loose, they discovered stable olivium, and all bets are off."

Uneasy, McAddis sighed. "Those colonists are in for a shock with people like the Rassua prowling around."

Keller peered at the reflection of Zoa's stiff face in the polished rim of the number-two scanner. "Naw, she's just going out there to open a young ladies' academy. Zoa's Charm School and Small Engine Repair."

Though he managed to get chuckles out of the two other men, that was all the relief they would get. On the engineering console, across the sci-deck from where the three men huddled, the severe-malfunction lights came on with a corresponding alarm. An instant later, half the board exploded in what was obviously not another hit, but internal damage finally blowing.

While Hahn pulled the leather-strapped presence of Zoa out of the way, Keller stumbled to the unmanned engineering console and tried to make sense of the flashing and smoldering. "Tetragrid overload! We need an engineer on the bridge to lock down the static pulses!"

"I'll do it," Hahn volunteered. He skimmed down the ladder, dropped to the lower deck, and crossed to the tactical boards.

Keller fought to tie his controls in to the tactical, racing the damage before it caused a calamity. "Starboard PTCs read amber!"

"Leave 'em alone!" Hahn turned briefly toward aft to make sure he was heard over the mechanical whine. "Cool those plasma injectors right now! Try the—"

The ship slammed sideways, driving Keller first backward, and then elbow-first into the environmental grids. The enemy had found them again and struck them in the main section's port side, hitting the skin of the cruiser mere feet from the bridge. A tumor of smoke and shrapnel burst out of the tactical displays.

The blast swallowed Derek Hahn completely. The last thing Keller saw of him was the wedge of his chin as the explosion struck him in the back.

"Oh, cripe—!" Keller was down the steps before he realized he was on his feet.

"Out of the way!" Roger Lake shoved Helmsman Makarios right out of his seat and plowed to Hahn.

He and Keller met at the first officer's writhing form. Lake pulled from one side, and Keller caught Hahn as they rolled him over.

Hahn's uniform was actually sizzling in Keller's hands, but the exo was conscious, talking, and trying to stand.

"I'm all right," Hahn gasped. "The injectors—"

"Pick him up." Lake pushed off the deck and veered back to the helm. "Blanket the phasers! Set up a grid and open fire!"

"Our weapons are depleting," Keller reminded, but it was like talking to a tree. "Blanketing shots without a target just wastes power!"

Derek Hahn reached out. "Roger!"

The captain didn't honor them with a response, turning instead to the frightened helm crew. "Ahead, quarter impulse!"

"Oh, no—" Hahn pressed a hand to Keller's knee and forced himself to his feet.

When Hahn stood up, Keller was choked by a heart-clutching sight of Hahn's uniform and the three inches of metal sticking out of the first officer's back on the right side, an unidentified piece of the blown board material.

Three inches out—how far in?

And how could he avoid a panic? He grasped Hahn from behind. "Captain, permission to drag Mr. Hahn kicking and screaming to sickbay?"

"What?" Hahn belched. "Get your hands off me!"

"Granted!"

"Come on, Derek." Looping an arm around the first officer, Keller hoisted him to the turbolift vestibule. Overhead, one leg pressed against the balcony rail, Tim McAddis stared down at them in a momentary lapse from the science boards.

He and Keller locked gazes for a moment. "Be right back, Tim," Keller undergirded.

The turbolift doors parted and he pulled Hahn inside. Hahn tried to help, but only one leg was working. Instead the exo clasped Keller's arms and shrieked, "It's the methane! Roger!"

"Hush," Keller warned, "don't make me rope you," and pulled him all the way in. The lift doors gushed closed, but before Keller could grasp the destination controller, Hahn collapsed against him and Keller devoted both hands to holding him.

Valiantly Hahn braced his legs and tried to stay upright, but slipped a centimeter with every agonized gasp. "He's snapping! Did you see—his—eyes?"

"It's just Gamma Night," Keller said. "He's never fought like this before."

"We shouldn't be moving—not a foot, not an inch, they—could lay mines in front of us—If we move, we're easier to find even on blinded sensors. It's the methane, Nick, I know it is—I know it is!"

Still holding him, Keller cranked halfway around. Where was the control arm? There! He gave it a twist. The mechanism felt sluggish in his hand. "Sickbay," he said.

Though the confirm light went on, the lift did nothing. Outside the closed doors, he could hear the action on the bridge and wanted to go back. The wound in Hahn's back was now bleeding into the fabric of Keller's sleeve, almost the same color.

"Sickbay!" he shouted at the sound-sensitive panel. "Dang box of rocks—"

Responding this time, the lift started to move downward, then chunked under his feet to a sudden dead stop and threw him and Hahn against the wall. Hahn gasped out his pain, and the lift began to descend again.

Less than ten feet down, the whole cab shifted a good two inches, tilted at a noticeable angle, and jammed to another grating stop.

"The guides!" Hahn choked out.

Keller looked up at the flashing warning lights. "Must be bent."

"If he'd sit still, the sensors might be able to pull in something. Open the doors—I've got to get back in there."

But Keller pressed him down, feeling desperation and his own fears rushing through his arms. "You sit still."

He craned around to look at the lift's control panel. How could he get it moving? The doors were jammed. There'd been a power surge.

"Did you see him?" Hahn coiled his arms around his own body. "He's not acting right. We don't need to be moving. We survived the surprise attack. We can stand toe to toe with anybody—there's nobody—read the reports—who can stand up to a destroyer point-blank in this sector. But if we're moving we can collide, we can hit anything else that's out there, our own thrusters and shields muck up our sensors . . ."

Maybe he was babbling, except that people who babble don't usually make perfect sense. Keller nodded in frustration and unhappy agreement, then broke the panel off the wall and got to the direct-feed cables. A puff of gray acid smoke piled out at him, souring the air in the lift. When it cleared, he looked into the panel opening. What he saw in there—he didn't even want to touch it, never mind stick his arm all the way in.

"Fused," he reported, more to himself than Hahn. "We're stuck."

"They'll break us—out in a minute." On the deck, Hahn's breathing grew more labored and his voice weaker. "I was hoping we could make it to Belle Terre. . . . Captain Kirk could take over . . . situation . . ." He pressed a bloody hand to his side again, but couldn't reach the wound in his back. As his head dropped against the lift wall, his waxy eyes beseeched Keller's. "We're overpaying our debt, Nick."

More concerned about Hahn than the lift, Keller divided his mind and knelt beside the injured officer, seeing their four years together dancing in front of his eyes.

Hahn grimaced and arched against the lift wall. "I—feel it now—I feel it—!" Pain twisted through him. He clutched toward the wound he couldn't possibly reach. "Is there something in me? I feel something solid. Pull it out!"

"There's nothing in there," Keller lied. "You're just ship-kicked."

Drunk with blood loss, Hahn couldn't raise his head. His eyes began to glaze. "He'll be poisoned. . . . Tavola exposure—you know what that means . . . but he saved our asses. Don't tell them, Nick . . . he'll cover for you. I will too . . ."

Stunned, Keller held his breath a few seconds before he realized what was happening. He dug his fingers into the chest placket of Hahn's uniform and shook him. "Derek, that was three years ago! Come out of it!"

"What?" Hahn murmured. His eyes cleared with a surge of adrenaline. "Oh, sorry . . . took a trip, didn't I?"

Angry now, Keller snapped, "Tavolo exposure shows itself in the first ninety days—you know that!"

"*Usually*," Hahn gagged. "And usually the person's watched like a hawk by every doctor within a light-year. Nick, he's snapping and it's our—"

"No, no," Keller insisted, feeling himself sweat under his jacket. This couldn't be rearing its ugly skull, could it? Not now! "He hasn't been in battle in over six years. It's just stress."

Forcing a shake of his head, Hahn argued, "The pressure's bringing the reaction out. We can't protect him anymore . . . We made a hell of a mistake. Today we . . . we pay."

From above, a faint voice filtered through the sound-muffling insulation. "Nick?"

Keller bolted to his feet. "Savannah! The lift's jammed! Break us out! We need help!"

A response thrummed through the shaft, but he couldn't make it out. For a moment he wondered how Savannah Ring had made it onto the bridge, but then his head cleared some and he remembered the companionway ladder leading down to the next deck. Then they must know the lift wasn't working.

"Open up the hatch," Hahn said. "Let's get back to the bridge."

"You're going to sickbay," Keller said. At least he could do that much.

"Till I get back," Hahn gasped, "keep our shields up, no matter what."

"If we run with full shields, the sensors won't work at all." Keller tried pushing at the ceiling hatch. The twisted lift must have jammed the hatch too. It wouldn't budge. "Not even the little bit of data we get trickling in—dang crippled thing, open up!"

Hahn flinched at the protest and grasped Keller's leg. "We shouldn't be running at all! Roger's cracking . . . you watch him. I—I—can't breathe . . ." His eyes cramped shut and he slipped sideways, his face a twisted knot.

Abandoning the hatch as he heard noises thunking from above, Keller quickly knelt again and pulled Hahn up, then yanked open the placket to loose the exo's jacket. "Let's get your belt off."

"You always—wanted an excuse—to get out of uniform. . . ."

Keller tried a grin. "At least the new ones have pockets in the britches. The other ones were just fancy PJs. What's a cowboy to do with his thumbs?"

"Still got those wranglers on . . ."

"Don't give me grief about m'boots. You don't outrank me that much."

"Nick—" Hahn fought his way back from the edge of consciousness again, battled down the pain that obviously had him by the body, and hooked his bloody hand on Keller's neck. "Nick, listen. It's time, it's time."

"Now, Dee," Keller moaned. "He's got thirteen years' command experience. That's better than what you and I got between us, even if he's a little shook."

"We let it go too long," Hahn wheezed. His gaze was now shockingly lucid. "As soon as I get back from sickbay," he vowed, "I'm relieving him."

More roughly than he meant, Keller tightened his grip. "Sit still. Let me get us out of here. Everything'll be better in a few minutes. Just sit."

On thready legs he stood again, reached up, and tried pulling on the hatch instead of pushing. The hatch squawked and moved this time, but it was meant to push out, not pull in, and the rim wouldn't give. "Come on, bust open," he grumbled. "What've I ever done to you?"

If only he had something to stand on, he could apply his weight onto the hatch with a well-arranged elbow. Muffled thunks and rasping of tools and metal told him they were breaking through from the bridge. He wanted to call out for them to hurry, but the lift tube was clustered with electrical outlets and access points that might be hot, dangerous. They couldn't hurry. He braced his legs and tried to push straight upward, but his boot heel skidded on the deck. His leg slipped out from under him. He staggered.

He looked down.

Hahn's blood painted the deck, a red smear across the lift floor, with a slashing imprint of the heel of Keller's left ranch boot.

Maybe if he'd wear regulation footwear, none of this would be happening. If one decision had been different somewhere way back—

Derek had tried to tell him. Why hadn't they made a different decision three years ago? Why couldn't they go back and fix it?

Below him, Derek Hahn sucked a lump of air and wheezed it back out. "The crew . . ."

"What about 'em?" Aggravated and taking it out on the hatch, Keller pushed harder on the stubborn panel.

There was no response this time. After a few seconds, the silence made sense.

"Derek?" Keller knelt again.

Hahn's eyes had lost their focus. Though sweat trailed down his face, his lips were relaxed now, his arms resting on his thighs. A breath gurgled in . . . out.

"Derek! They're almost through!"

Though the first officer was still breathing, he no longer blinked or responded. His eyelids began to sag, his tight facial muscles to go limp. His face turned pasty. Another choked breath clawed its way in.

Terror seized Keller by the heart. This was supposed to be a milk run. An easy mission. A six-month flight out to Belle Terre, the same heading all the way, boring, quiet, peaceful, simple, then take over picket duty at Belle Terre and relieve the *Enterprise* to return to Federation space.

Suddenly everything shattered around him like a glass bulb he held too tight in his hand. His fingers crushed the bulb into ever-smaller shards.

Something thumped on the lift roof. The access hatch cranked open with a ghastly shriek. Bent metal, crying, weeping.

There it was. The way back to the bridge. A hand came down.

Whose?

Look for STAR TREK fiction from Pocket Books

Star Trek®: The Original Series

Star Trek: The Next Generation®

Star Trek: Voyager®

Star Trek®: The Captain's Table

Star Trek®: The Dominion War

Star Trek®: The Badlands

Star Trek® Books available in Trade Paperback

STAR TREK
THE EXPERIENCE
LAS VEGAS HILTON

Be a part of the most exciting deep space adventure in the galaxy as you beam aboard the U.S.S. Enterprise. Explore the evolution of Star Trek® from television to movies in the "History of the Future Museum," the planet's largest collection of authentic Star Trek memorabilia. Then, visit distant galaxies on the "Voyage Through Space." This 22-minute action packed adventure will capture your senses with the latest in motion simulator technology. After your mission, shop in the Deep Space Nine Promenade and enjoy 24th Century cuisine in Quark's Bar & Restaurant.

- -

Save up to $30